MANFISHING

Dedicated to Doreen

*

MANFISHING

Trials and triumphs in the realm of the local rag

PETER PHEASANT

Pete Pheasant

NOVEMBER 2024

DB
PUBLISHING

First published 2024 by DB Publishing, an imprint of JMD Media Ltd,

Nottingham, United Kingdom.

Copyright © 2024, Peter Pheasant

ISBN 9781780916620

Printed in the UK

CHAPTER ONE

1

SIMON Fox lit the remains of last night's spliff and inhaled the view from Sandy Ridge. Much of the *Brexham Bugle*'s circulation area was visible from this ancient outcrop, where generations of children had climbed Everest and couples had carved their everlasting love.

Wisps of factory smoke punctuated a sweep of housing that began on one side of the Harford Valley with a burgeoning Wimpey development and ended on the other with a postwar council estate.

Nineteenth-century industrial prosperity had draped a grey blanket in the middle: slate-topped rows of two-up-two-down terrace houses that now squinted through double-glazed windows and spluttered over exhaust fumes. The old pitmen's houses fell away to playing fields fringed by paint sprayers, breakers' yards and pigeon lofts to the west and a railway line to the east.

A toytown industrial estate of small firms going up and big firms coming down marked the end of civilisation as Brexham knew it.

Beyond lay the flooded valley floor, where opencast workings had long given way to swans and herons. Sunlight danced on its waters and darted among the defiant shards of glass in the Morbury Viaduct, a giant brick monument to Victorian engineering, its mighty shoulders once the bearer of grand steam trains, its ragged armpits now home to gluesniffers and walk-me-home sex in the ruined tenements where rail workers once slept to the lullaby of the loco.

It wasn't paradise, Simon thought, but it would do.

Beyond him stretched the waters of his world, teeming with men-fish waiting to be caught on his journalistic line: a world so rich in characters with tales to tell and secrets to hide that, whenever thoughts of fame and Fleet Street crossed his mind, any attempt at comparison seemed futile. All he could want was here.

From this vantage point, an ugly streak of cleared land on the other side of the town centre did not impinge on the vista, though it played a significant role in his working life.

The hint of sadness in his eyes today, however, stemmed from matters of the heart, for as he swept back the ginger curls that reached the shoulders of a pale paisley shirt, he pictured his mother, lying in a hospital bed with a bag in place of the bladder taken from her by cancer.

With a silent prayer to the god he did not believe in, he checked the pockets of his two-tone brown Budgie jacket for cigarettes, lighter and tinfoil pack of cheese and Marmite sandwiches, slung it over one shoulder and set off for the offices of the weekly newspaper where he had trained as a reporter and qualified on the modest sum of £30 a week.

A gangling 5ft 11in in John Lennon specs, cotton flares and desert boots, he cut a familiar figure as he strolled dreamily down the gently sloping High Street with the voice of TV racing commentator Peter O'Sullevan crackling in his head:

'And they're off. And Fox is taking an early lead. As they go into the straight, passing Skinheads' Corner, the conditions are almost perfect.

'There's Big-Breasted Lady ahead, then comes Councillor Claire with "Morning Simon" and making a promising run is Frazzled Mum of Three out of Timothy Whites, trained by Pampers.

'Over the potholes we go and Geordie John's calling "Watcyha Scoop" from "Spuds, Best Red" on the market side, and making a good run on the right with a discreet nod and dull colours is Municipal Treasurer.

'Three furlongs to go and it's "Ey up, youth" from Car Thief, with Mrs Women's Institute coming up on the inside. We've five in contention now and Stammering Mark's a-waving from the ironmonger's.

'Smiling Sue Estate Agent is showing well, there's Grunted Greeting from PC Clay, "How's it going?" from Butcher Tom, "Thanks for the write-up" from Playgroup Leader and "Don't forget our anniversary Sunday" from Methodist Minister.'

*

IT was only half past eight but the unseasonal heat of this May morning in 1976 had glued the shirt to his back by the time he neared a small crowd outside the *Bugle* office, which looked as it had for decades, its large window etched with the newspaper's name in red in the same old serif typeface that formed its masthead.

An elderly woman was lying in the road, her legs partially under a taxi, her head resting on a coat. An anxious young man was holding her hand and telling anyone who would listen, 'She just stepped out in front of me.'

Roy Dunne, the *Bugle*'s junior reporter of three, moved among the watching ghouls, hurriedly taking notes.

Simon slipped down the alleyway connecting the newspaper office to Solly's Transport Café and Gentlemen's Lodging House.

Inside the bay-windowed Edwardian building that was once home to the *Bugle*'s founding editor, reporter Gary Bostock emerged grinning from the glorified cupboard that passed as office library and store room.

'Missed all the action, have I? What a pity. Is she dead?'

'As compassionate as ever, I see, Mr Bostock!' Simon snorted.

The newsroom door flew open and two proud sideburns and a noisy kipper tie appeared, wearing a slightly overweight and prematurely balding man in his late 30s.

'Jesus!' Simon laughed. 'Pass the sunglasses.'

Colin Goodacre joined in with the laughter, jiggling his glasses Eric Morecambe-style and straightening the latest horror from his tie rack, with its palm trees and parrots.

'Watch it, sunshine,' he said, 'if you ever get to sit in my seat, you'll have to wear one of these.

'Now,' he continued with a let's-get-on-with-it rub of the hands, 'you doing the crash, Roy? Shout up if you need any help, mate, and keep checking the lady's condition. They'll take her to Norton General, I'd imagine, and the staff there are pretty good with updates.'

'Er, dunno if you think this might be interesting, boss,' Roy said nervously, 'but they're all talking outside about the new road, saying this wouldn't have happened if the old ones weren't so busy.'

'Huh! That old chestnut,' Simon scoffed. 'Accidents just happen, you know.'

'True, but it might give us a new line,' the editor said. 'Get some for-and-against quotes about the road, Roy. It's always a good talking point. Now then, Gary's on sport, which leaves you with the bits and bobs, Simon, my old flower.'

He held out a wad of press releases and readers' letters, lingering long enough to savour the grimace that greeted the top sheet: Brexham and District Chess Club's weekly report, a tortuous missive that was routinely cut to four paragraphs as a news page filler, since the editor's ruling that it could not possibly go in the sports section, because chess involved neither sweating nor special clothing.

Before long, the newsroom echoed to the clatter of ancient typewriters being pounded by two-fingered typists seated side by side at a worktop that spanned the former dining room of the paper's founder, whose bearded ghost was said to haunt the premises.

So cluttered was the communal desk with notebooks, filing trays, newspapers, ashtrays and telephones that reporters had developed a way of typing with their elbows high. Every now and then a burst of inspiration was signalled by keys being struck with extra ferocity.

It was Tuesday morning, the half-hour point in Colin's clock, midway between publications. Back at his desk he flicked through the eight sheets of A4 paper that represented managing director Walter Harding's imitation of the week's broadsheet pages in miniature, and sighed.

Barely a dozen adverts were drawn in and it would be Thursday morning, hours from deadline, before Walter's estate agent friends had decided how much space they wanted. By then, the journalists might have produced far too many stories or nowhere near enough.

The editor did a rough count: 80-odd columns of news to fill at 22 inches per column equalled about 50 yards of text. Not bad value for 9p, he reckoned. Then he looked at the typewritten list of articles he had read, edited and headlined so far. They would fill less than half the potential news space.

He needed light relief and pulled a battered folder from his drawer, found the page headed 'Stranger than fiction' and allowed himself a good-job-they've got-me-in-charge smile as he ran a finger down the collection of howlers gleaned from reporters' copy: the parish councillors calling for pedestrian *refugees* on a busy road, the principal *guset* at a club dinner, the theft of a *blue girl's* bicycle, the man arrested over drugs *found by police hidden in his underpants*.

At precisely 9.30am, Walter Harding's cardigan announced its presence in the newsroom. It was the red one with leather buttons. When Walter passed on to the great printworks in the sky, his cardigans would surely be recorded in the Deaths column.

Walter's bowels were the best alarm clock known to man. Each morning at the same time, they led the slightly stooped figure of the managing director on his weary shuffle from an office piled high with notes to himself and dusty ledgers at the front of the building to the gents' toilet at the back.

Generations of *Bugle* reporters, heads hung in concentration over typewriters or ears glued to phones, had glimpsed Walter's cardigan or caught a whiff of his pipe and realised they had better get a move on if they were to catch the opening session at the magistrates' court, where lawyers for businessmen caught drink-driving or fiddling their VAT returns would try to slip their cases through before the press arrived.

Worse still was the knowledge that if Walter beat his staff to the loo, they would have to clench their buttocks for half an hour before he re-emerged from the tiny cubicle, by now thick with the smoke of Light Shag.

How Walter spent his time there, day after day without a book or a newspaper, was a source of endless speculation by the reporters, as, indeed, was the way he managed to fill his working week so slothfully, yet survive so long as the man in charge of a pillar of the local community.

It was not only when lit that Walter's pipe was a weapon to fear. Occasionally, as he rested his stomach against the back of a reporter's chair, chattering idly as his victim typed frantically in the hope that he would go away, the pipe hung from the corner of pinched lips and a runaway globule of saliva raced down the stem, re-grouped at the base of the bowl and ended its yo-yo journey with a splodge on the reporter's shoulder.

Walter had never been to charm school.

Young newshounds, their bellies full of fire, looked at him and despaired. With Walter at the helm, where on earth was the paper heading? They cared not that his steadiness, his very ordinariness, had endeared him to the owners, two elderly brothers who rarely visited the office, let alone interfered in matters of editorial content, and who asked little more from their family inheritance than a monthly cheque in the post.

And yet, when forced into areas of conflict, Walter was a resolute defender of the *Bugle*'s right to publish what it saw fit, so long as it was fair and accurate, no matter how it might offend advertisers or the powers that be. 'We're a NEWSpaper,' he would say with finality, and for that, editors down the years had endured low pay and the trappings of Dickensianism that dogged the paper to the present day.

Walter's admin staff might have been hand-picked for curiosity value.

Mrs P, who wore a pink mitten to conceal a deformed left hand, looked after the accounts and toilet rolls. The latter had once triggered a crisis meeting with Walter over the reporters' excessive use of Andrex, prompting the MD to warn that he would bring back Izal if they did not mend their ways, adding, with a chuckle, that they should need only three sheets per visit: one to wipe, one to clean and one to polish.

Celia Staunton and Katie Tummins ran the reception desk, and an odd-job man named Joe spent two hours every Friday with a Woodbine between his lips as he cleaved photographic metal plates from their wooden mountings and tossed them into a box for recycling.

A nervous affliction made Celia's head jerk from side to side. So timid was she that the very idea of saying boo to a goose had never occurred to her.

Thirty years' service had left Celia in charge of the string, sticky labels and envelopes with which the office junior parcelled up reporters' copy, photographs and page layouts twice a day for dispatch by a No 54 bus, whose fleet number and estimated time of arrival he must phone through to the printers five miles away, knowing that if he forgot, it might be 24 hours before they caught up with the bus and the week's production schedule would be in tatters.

Beak-nosed and Jimmy Hill-chinned, Katie harboured a manic giggle that burst forth at inappropriate moments. For 364 days of the year, her unrequited lust was locked away but, come the Christmas fuddle, she would tonsil-fish whichever reporter she could lay her hands on, to whoops of delight from his workmates.

Katie's duties included refilling pots of glue from a gallon drum so that hand-written announcements of births, deaths, marriages, golden wedding anniversaries, driving test passes, appeals for picture postcards and prewar sideboards, discounts on farmyard manure, thank-yous and best wishes, dancing diplomas, tote numbers, plumbers for hire, jumble sales and declarations by deserted husbands that they were no longer liable for their wives' debts, could be pasted on to regulation paper fit for a typesetter's clipboard and delivered to a waiting world.

As Simon collected a Women's Institute report from Reception, he paused to grimace at the throng of customers in a hurry but forced to play by the rules of this dilatory duo: a PR nightmare, perhaps, but as much a part of the newspaper as the rising stars of the newsroom with their red-hot exclusives.

It was a humbling thought that, long after young reporters and their tales of political scandals and bureaucratic bungling had come and gone, the *Bugle*'s army of readers would still be remembering dates and events that truly mattered and telling each other about them in their own way through the 4p-a-word Classifieds columns.

2

ALL Brexham had to show for 20 years of talking was a trail of destruction.

The dream of a new road through this small Midlands town emerged in the boom years of 1950s Britain. Car ownership was rising rapidly and residential roads were becoming congested.

But as time dragged on, the plan for three-quarters of a mile of dual carriageway running parallel to High Street became a political football.

Although the grandly named Brexham Town Centre Traffic Corridor was a county council project, the borough council was responsible for rehousing residents displaced by demolition to clear the route. And it was at this lower level, closer to grass-roots opinion, that doubts slowly turned into outright opposition.

Critics argued that feeding thousands of vehicles into a cutting at one end of the town and spitting them out at the other, cloaking houses and shops with pollution along the way, made no sense when old railway lines on the outskirts lay unused.

Tory support for the project remained strong but Labour doubts hardened, and there was no fiercer critic than Frank Noon, a firebrand union official and rising star of the party.

In any other town, the county council might have steamrollered the scheme through. But the area was notoriously prone to swings at election time and, as voting for the two authorities took place two years apart, neither party could plan with certainty.

The government had no desire to get involved in a local spat and, with road schemes elsewhere vying for attention, Brexham's never climbed high enough up

Westminster's list of priorities to guarantee funding.

The result was a slowly growing snake of cleared land as dozens of homes and small businesses were bought up and demolished.

Old folk, happy in their damp, cramped little cottages, with communal back yards, where everybody knew each other, found themselves shipped off to an out-of-town estate with no community facilities and a single shop whose Asian owners had given up combating graffiti since 'I LOVE INGLND' had appeared in foot-high letters on its shutters.

By the spring of 1976, the bulldozers had reached Pinder Terrace at the southern tip of the route. And there they met Annie Shaw.

Annie owned the two-up, two-down cottage she called her little palace and had no intention of going anywhere, not without a good price - and a council flat close to the town centre.

'I'll lie down in front of the bulldozers,' she vowed in a Bugle interview that sparked a flurry of media interest, even attracting radio and TV stations.

'Four foot ten and six stone wet through,' in her words, Annie was in her early 60s but spunky as a teenager. She typified the townsfolk Simon Fox had grown to love: gritty, pragmatic, proud of their town, yet scathing about its shortcomings (that being their prerogative and theirs alone); conservative in their socialism; hard to get to know, then welcoming as hot soup on a bleak seafront; rarely appeased once crossed but for ever loyal to those they trusted.

The sort who would never dream of calling a spade a long-handled, flat-bladed digging implement.

One side of Pinder Terrace had by now been demolished. The facing terrace of nine cottages remained, six of them empty and awaiting demolition. Norman Hartshorne's corner shop stood at one end, with Annie's place in the middle, two doors from the rented home of an elderly double amputee named Tommy Jepson.

Norman told anyone who would listen, 'They'll have to carry me out in a box.' Tommy's fate was in the hands of a landlord he had never met, and life was about to become uncomfortable.

3

BUILT like a garden rake, Flick rolled off the stained settee where he had spent the night in his caravan home in his parents' garden and stumbled to the tiny bathroom, massaging his crotch with the hand tattooed with a swastika in loving memory of 'Paki-bashing' raids in Leicester. It was gone 1pm.

Shane 'Flick' Beresford had earned his nickname from an argument involving a knife and a fellow schoolboy's face.

In later years, he won trophies for his dancefloor acrobatics at soul discos, dressed to perfection in Stay-Prest and Ben Sherman. With his blond locks and piercing blue eyes, he could have any girl he wanted, and did.

Then he discovered amphetamines.

He peered through the spiderish cracks of the bathroom mirror at a prune-faced, gap-toothed skinhead of 30 going on 60 and laughed.

''Andsome bastard!'

Splashing his face with cold water, he winced as he caught a scab above his right eye, a souvenir of a few days earlier, when he had spent the early afternoon getting drunk in the Cobblers' Arms before taking an abandoned supermarket trolley for a ride down High Street and crashing into a shop wall.

The incident had made two paragraphs in the *Bugle*. Shoppers watched in horror, the paper said, as the trolley narrowly missed a bus. But Flick was well aware of his reputation. He suspected they watched more in hope.

One sharp whistle brought Monty bounding from his basket and into his master's arms.

'C'mon, my beauty!' Flick laughed, looking into the whippet's eyes and kissing it full on the lips before setting out to walk the mile or so into town, Monty tugging hard on the length of rope attached to his collar

Flick had an appointment at the police station. His sister Tracey had whispered a message to him while visiting their folks with her little one, Lucy.

He stopped off at the Cobblers' and ordered a pint of Shipstone's bitter. The jukebox was blaring out Black Sabbath's *Paranoid* as he found a quiet corner and began apparently sobbing into his hands. Soon a group of young hardnuts-in-waiting and dolled-up schoolgirls had gathered around, asking what was wrong and doling out sympathy and cigarettes as Flick explained that his dear old mum had died and he didn't know how he could carry on living.

It went like a dream, until an old-timer at the bar asked what all the fuss was about and the barmaid explained.

'Bloody queer, that,' said the old man in a voice audible across the room. 'I've just seen Mrs Beresford in t'butcher's.'

Showered with boos and beer, Flick bundled Monty into his arms and sped for the exit door. He was still laughing when he reached the police station.

The desk clerk led him to an upstairs room, where Detective Inspector Jim 'Richo' Richardson was waiting beside his office door. 'Ah, Mr Beresford!' he boomed for the benefit of prying ears. 'I hear you might have some information for me?'

Closing the door behind them, the inspector beckoned Flick to take a seat, pulled on a rubber glove, reached into a drawer and handed over a small brown envelope. Inside were two £10 notes and a piece of blotting paper with two circular marks that Fick recognised instantly as LSD.

'Now,' the detective all but whispered, 'earn it.'

The thought of protesting flashed through Flick's mind. He was not big on scruples but terrorising an old man made him uneasy.

As if reading his thoughts, the inspector leaned across his desk and growled, 'Just make sure the old bloke knows he's no longer safe living there, understand? You fucked it up last time. Don't do it again – not unless you want your dad to find out your dirty secret.'

Twenty quid was half a week's wage for his labouring pals and, as Flick left the cloying atmosphere of the nick, his conscience lost its voice. He took Monty for a long walk to kill time before reaching the Unicorn Inn, where man and mutt shared three pints of mild and a cheese and onion roll until darkness descended.

Then they threaded their way through the rubble of a demolition site, where Flick paused to pick up a large boulder and headed for Pinder Terrace, with its solitary street light.

4

SATURDAY was just one more working day for the *Bugle*'s reporters and Simon had a church garden party to cover. But first he was dropping in on Mrs Shaw.

'Ooh, look what t'cat's dragged in!' a pint-sized figure with tight-cropped grey hair shrieked from the kitchen sink as he appeared at the window.

'Come on in, lad, and don't mind me, I'm only kiddin'. People say I've gorra gob the size of next wick. Gets me into no end o' trouble, yer know.'

He hugged her gently.

'But I sez to 'em,' Annie continued breathlessly, 'I sez, life's too short to be miserable. You 'ave to 'ave a laugh while you can, don't you? Now, go through, lad, and make yersen comfy. I'm just mashin'. Fancy a cuppa and a cream cake?'

'Well,' he looked at his watch, 'I really ought to...'

'Course yer do!' Annie laughed and ushered him into her polished front room, where Tommy Jepson was in his wheelchair, watching racing on the telly.

Tommy had featured in the *Bugle* several times because of his charity fundraising and Simon had got to know him well. The old man had lost both legs below the knee but his warmth and humour had never waned.

''Ello, old son,' he smiled ''Ow's yer mam gettin' on?'

'Ooh, not bad, Tommy, thanks,' the reporter lied. 'But what are *you* doing here?'

'I reckon,' Tommy's voice rose, 'I've met the woman o' me dreams, only I don't know as she'll 'ave me.' Then, in an old man's whisper, 'I've come to mend a plug for 'er but don't say owt, you know 'ow funny she is.'

'Is 'e talking mucky again?' Annie said, tea tray tinkling in raspberry-ripple hands. "E's a dirty owd bugger – and that's swearin'!'

'But my pet,' Tommy feigned hurt, 'I told you times many, we could make such sweet music, me 'n' thee. Just let me get yer on t'dancefloor.'

And with that he pushed his torso up with his elbows and disco-danced with his stumps.

It was eight years since the last amputation but there were times when Tommy could still feel his toes.

'Anyway,' he said, his big, round face crimson with mirth below a full head of flaxen hair, 'I told you I only lost two o' me legs.'

'Ooh, 'ark at 'im! You'll make the young man blush,' Annie said, making the young man blush. 'An' don't you "pet" me, Tommy Jepson. Anyroad,' she added, an upper arm pushing up what would have been the breast she'd lost to cancer, 'I've told you I'm only 'alf a woman.'

'That's all right then, 'cause I'm only 'alf a man.'

Simon could have listened to this comedy duo all day but finished his cake and tea and made to leave.

'Any news on the move, Annie?' he asked.

'Not a word. But,' turning to Tommy, 'you've 'ad some news, 'aven't you?'

'Oh? Good news, Tommy?'

'Someone's trying to drive 'im out of 'is 'ouse,' Annie huffed. 'Wicked, it is. Tell 'im, Tommy.'

'I dunna want to say owt,' the old man scowled, 'not yet.'

'Fair enough,' said Simon. 'Let me know if I can help, though. And take care of yourselves, you two.'

He was barely out of the door when Annie admonished her neighbour, 'Yer need to stand up for yersen, Tommy Jepson.'

'What, and let every thieving toerag in t'neighbourhood know I'm a sitting duck? Owd man wi' no legs livin' alone on a deserted street? Leave it alone, pet.'

*

TOMMY had found the boulder in the bathroom that morning. It must have come through the window as he slept.

An earlier attack had left him with a boarded-up kitchen window for two weeks. He had put that down to boyish mischief but this one had unsettled him enough to call the police, though he expected no swifter action from them than from Gerald Tooms, the oily lettings agent for Pinder Housing, which Tommy always thought was a rather pompous name for an enterprise that, to his knowledge, owned just one house and belonged to the invisible 'Miss Wolverson'.

Tooms answered the call with a promise to fix the window as soon as possible, though he couldn't commit to a date.

Funny that, Tommy thought; he was never late collecting the rent.

Woman Police Constable Wendy Marshall's arrival within the hour surprised him almost as much as her appearance. ('Just a slip of a lass,' he would tell Annie later. 'You'd never think she'd sort out tap-room brawlers on a Friday night but I suppose she can handle 'ersen.')

He insisted on serving the young officer tea and custard cream biscuits and told her about the earlier vandalism and the revolting parcel that had come through his letterbox shortly afterwards.

Stepping into the rear garden, she pointed to an open gateway at the far end, where a public alleyway ran along the back of the terrace.

'So, this must be where they threw the bricks from, Mr Jepson?'

'Aye – and less of the Mr Jepson, mi duck,' he chuckled. 'It's Tommy, or Tom if you prefer. I'm not proud.'

'Fair enough, Tommy,' she smiled. 'I guess they just wandered in off the alley. And I see you've not got a gate.'

'There were one at one time but it got nicked, for scrap, I guess. They'll pinch owt round 'ere.'

'Bit more brazen with the parcel through the front door, though.'

'Huh!' Tommy scowled. 'No one's gonna catch 'em, though, are they? It's like a ghost town 'ere. We're sitting ducks for anyone up to no good.'

She gave him a hug and promised to keep an eye on the neighbourhood whenever she could.

'Aye, well, good luck wi' that,' Tommy said, adding that in his day, the fear of being clipped around the ear by a burly bobby before going home to a thrashing from one's dad was enough to keep all but the unruliest of youths in check.

*

AT the age of 72, Tommy viewed life with a wry smile.

Twenty years of toiling at the coal face had left him relatively unscathed but his legs were no match for the lorry that ran over him as he returned from work one night and an overtaking car clipped his moped, sending him into the trucker's path.

Rose had warned him not to get 'that blasted machine' but he wouldn't listen. There was, however, one who did listen, as Rose would tell family and friends in the months and years to come: the one who answered her prayers as her husband hovered between life and death.

And when at last Tommy returned home, it was to a Rose reborn, for ever cheerful as she washed and dressed him, heaved him around in his wheelchair and tucked him up in his new bed in the front room, while all the time tending to the mental wounds that cut deeper than the surgeon's knife. 'Cheer up, Tommy Jepson!' she'd chide as she sensed him sliding into depression. 'There's lots worse off than you.'

Rose taught him to laugh again and when a heart attack struck her down without warning, Tommy was in disbelief as much as grief. After all, he was a heavy-smoking atheist and lifelong drinker: it had seemed only natural that he would go first

He thought at first of moving out but Number 12 was where they had built and rebuilt their lives. And, with help from daughter Jean and her handyman husband Derek, some semblance of independence returned.

When news of the road scheme threatened the little cottage, Tommy asked himself what Rose would do, and had no doubts about the answer: he would stay put, until the council found him a flat or a bungalow near Jean's place. Or until the bulldozers were at his door.

Annie Shaw had been no more than 'that old battleaxe up the road' before Rose's death. But an unlikely friendship developed between the widowed pair, helping Tommy to glimpse light in his loneliness, though his true salvation was his workshop.

Derek had fixed it up for him, taking a former mess hut off British Rail's hands after his gang had been given a more modern facility. Derek single-handedly dismantled, transported and rebuilt it at the end of Tommy's garden, then fitted a strip light powered by an extension from a socket inside the house.

Tommy marvelled at his ingenuity. The hut was too big to fit facing the house, so Derek erected it sideways on, tight against the 3ft-high picket fence that separated the garden from the alleyway. Then he made a gentle ramp so that Tommy could reach the entrance from his path.

All it was missing was a door, the original having been smashed by burglars daft enough to think there might be something of value in a place where rail workers had their tea and sandwiches. But Derek found a door in a skip when workmen were renovating houses on his estate. He trimmed and hung it to perfection, happy that Tommy could lock his shed from inside and out.

'It's even got a letterbox, Tom,' he laughed. 'No flap, though – you'll have to tape it up sometime.'

Tommy never did.

There were days when he would shut himself away in the hut for hours, armed with beef dripping sandwiches and a flask of tea flavoured with whisky. In his solitude, new skills budded and blossomed, almost as if deprivation in one sense had brought strength in another. He became an accomplished woodworker.

From jewellery boxes made with iced-lolly sticks and lined with velvet, which he sold for charity at the miners' welfare, he graduated to window boxes and letter racks for friends and family, to cricket bats and stilts for the kids who played in Jean's street.

His biggest project to date was a bird table for Annie. She liked nothing more than to watch the birds in her garden. He aimed to have it finished in time for her birthday and could almost hear her now. 'You big, daft beggar, what do I want with that?' she'd say and make some excuse to go to the kitchen for a cry.

5

DETECTIVE Inspector Jim Richardson left his little secret sleeping soundly.

The bathroom mirror showed a handsome man of 41. Combing his thick, black hair and scraping a flake of skin from his nose, he ran both hands down his chest, smiling at the firmness. There was no disguising a slight paunch but that was hardly surprising, considering the time spent drinking with cops and crooks in the course of his work.

He placed a gentle kiss on the forehead of the woman young enough to be his daughter, slipped outside and drove back to the station with memories of their first meeting swimming through his head.

He had been representing the force at the launch of a new rail service linking Brexham and Birmingham and had enjoyed freeloading with fellow VIP guests, slugging champagne while balancing buffet food on paper plates served by an army of strawberry-suited PR girls.

By the time they were herded into the party suite with its thick carpets and sunken lights, the inspector had so warmed to his assignment that he offered little resistance when a petite young blonde whose name badge said 'Tracey, Marketing Assistant' pulled him into a giggling throng of civic dignitaries boogieing to the Bee Gees.

They danced and shouted through the music and laughed and scoffed from the sweet trolley and drank and danced some more until the tempo was turned down, with Stevie Wonder's *My Cherie Amour,* and he found himself crushed against her firm breasts, trying to put his hands anywhere but on her bottom and failing to hide the uncomfortable bulge in his trousers as he buried his reddening face in her silky, sweet hair.

'Inspector Richardson!' she whispered. 'Did you forget to leave your truncheon at home?'

'Sorry,' he stammered, 'Think it's time I sat down.'

'Shh. Meet me in ten minutes, two carriages down, far end,' she whispered, slipping out of his embrace and vanishing into the shadows.

The inspector strained to effect normality as he adjusted his tie, squeezed through jigging bodies and headed for a small table in the corner of the carriage, where he downed another glass of fizz.

As he checked his watch at the appointed time, swaying gently at the end of a corridor lit only by passing street lights, he wondered if he was being taken for a mug. This was like something from readers' letters in *Penthouse*.

There was no sign of her.

Then a hand grabbed his arm and pulled him through a half-open doorway, shush-ing as she led him towards a small sofa beside a coffee table

'What *is* this place,' he whispered, but her lips were already on his, hot and urgent.

'Staff rest room,' she giggled between kisses and felt for his belt.

In an instant, his hands were inside her blouse, her nipples stiffening against his thumbs.

Pushing her on to the sofa, he sank to his knees, eased back her skirt and nuzzled his face between her thighs, his erection throbbing angrily at the knowledge that she was not wearing knickers.

His tongue pierced the wet folds of her sex and she took control, grinding, gyrating until he thought he would suffocate as she covered his face with her juice.

He sensed her climax rising and pulled away, almost busting his zip as he yanked his pants down, then thrust into her, covering her moans with kisses and nibbles as bone met bone. He wanted to slow down but the train's rhythm was irresistible and he hammered into her like a schoolboy virgin as she arched and bucked, the heels of her shoes digging into his back.

Their absence apparently unnoticed, they slipped back into the hospitality suite shortly before the train reached its destination and parted with a professional handshake that concealed a note containing her phone number.

TRACEY'S cheeks would flush when they recalled that day in the months ahead. It was not, she insisted, something she had ever done before.

It did not take the inspector long to discover the truth about his 'bit on the side'. She was Shane 'Flick' Beresford's younger sister. She also had a young daughter.

Richardson would ask himself many times how this bright, clean, articulate woman could have emerged from such a grubby, worthless tribe, though he put it more delicately one afternoon during their weekly rendezvous at her one-bedroom flat.

'Well,' she laughed, 'the baby was a mistake, obviously. One fucking big mistake! I wanted to get rid of it at first. I was only 15, for chrissake! But Mam's a Catholic and would have none of it. And I'm glad now, of course. Anyway, soon as I turned 16, Mam arranged for me to go and stay with her sister in Skegness. They're chalk and cheese, Mam and Auntie Val, and Mam thought I'd have a better chance of making something for myself and Lucy if I didn't hang around Brexham.

'She was right an' all. Val was brilliant: put me through college, got her mate's PR firm to take me on and was dead keen to babysit while I was working. Then a vacancy came up at their office down here and she helped get me this place through the council.'

Slowly and against her better instincts, Tracey had found her feelings for the older man growing stronger. She knew it was mainly about sex for him but he was funny and considerate. He treated her with respect, so unlike her own uncouth father.

She felt her guard falling ever more easily in his company and, on one of the rare occasions when his wife had gone to stay with an old school friend and an afternoon of sex turned into evening cuddles and an overnight stay, she let slip her secret: Lucy's father was Tracey's brother.

Flick had let his sister join him and his friends one night in his caravan and, after several glasses of cider and a smoke of some pungent weed, Tracey had fallen asleep on the sofa. She awoke to find his friends gone and Flick inside her.

'Oh god!' she stared anxiously into the policeman's eyes. 'I should NOT have told you that. No one else knows. Mam and Dad tried to get it out of me but I wouldn't tell. Shane would've gone to prison, I guess.'

'Bloody hell, yeah! Incest at least, rape at worst.'

He pictured her father, Cyril Beresford, a well-known brawler in his youth and still a handful in his 50s when he'd had a drink too many and someone in a pub looked at him the wrong way.

'You mustn't ever tell Dad, Jim. Promise.'

*

THE spark had long since gone out of Jim and Eunice Richardson's marriage. The early days of lust and laughter had given way to a polite partnership. She kept house and ironed his shirts; his salary and the rent from 12 Pinder Terrace gave them a comfortable lifestyle and two weeks by the sea in summer.

They had hoped for children but, after years of trying, Eunice had been diagnosed with primary ovarian failure and her waning interest in sex had all but died with early-onset menopause. By then, Jim had risen through the police ranks and they had settled in a semi two miles out of town.

Sidney Wolverson had taken to his daughter's first serious boyfriend from the outset. It was good to have some male company after a lifetime with two mousy women. Jim seemed straight as a die but had an impish sense of humour and there was something about him that made Sidney think he would go far.

Athletic and well-dressed, he seemed a fine catch for the plain little girl Sidney had feared would be left on the shelf. He was well-spoken, too – 'for a Yorkshireman', he would tease – and when Sidney walked Eunice down the aisle, he was a proud and happy man, looking forward to the joys of grandchildren.

By the time pancreatic cancer took him at the age of 56, the wily accountant had made Eunice sole director of Pinder Housing and owner of its single asset, number 12. His hope was that it would provide the couple with a nest egg in retirement but he had put the company in her maiden name, just in case.

Sleeping around was many a policeman's lot in the '70s and Jim Richardson had enjoyed numerous little bonuses by the time he rose to detective inspector, though none as lingering as Tracey.

Sex aside, she made him laugh and they talked about everything, and nothing. He thought of running away with her, of giving Lucy a proper father and catching up on the joys of raising a child.

Running away was increasingly something he felt he had to do – from Brexham and its dying town centre and grubby estates; from its rising unemployment as cheap imports closed engineering and textile factories; from its growing underbelly of aimless young men and women seeking release in cannabis and amphetamines; from the petty burglars, shoplifting grannies and drunken wife-beaters who took up much of his time in the sure knowledge that locking them up would merely push them further down life's greasy pole.

Whether he would make his new future with Eunice or Tracey, or neither, he had yet to decide but he still had friends in his native Whitby, where the chief superintendent was his old pal Clive Pullman. 'When are you putting in for a transfer, Jim?' Pullman had written on his latest Christmas card. 'There's a better class of villain up here.'

Much as he dreamed of a fresh start amid sea air and dramatic scenery, Richardson was determined to broaden his options. That meant maximising his finances, and that meant selling the house at Pinder Terrace. But Eunice would not hear of selling Daddy's legacy until there was no alternative, until all the wrangling over the road had finished and demolition was inevitable. Or until old Mr Jepson found somewhere else to live.

'Anyway,' she would say, 'the road might never go ahead for all we know.'

That was his nightmare. Then they would be stuck with the house and one less reason to leave Brexham. Once the place became vacant, though, the council would have no choice but to buy it, since council plans had blighted any prospect of a resale. Similar houses nearby had gone for £7,000, double his copper's salary: a nice getaway ticket.

If only the old man could be persuaded to move.

The inspector would keep his promise to Tracey. For now. But he let Flick know that he knew his secret. He had no doubt that Flick feared his father's wrath even more than the stretch inside that he could expect if the fingerprints he had inadvertently left on the inspector's desk were somehow linked to an unsolved crime.

6

SIMON entered the hospital with a sense of doom that had grown in the weeks since his mother's second operation.

Lynne was with him, as always: his lover, his best friend, his rock. Slim, just 5ft 4in tall, but a giant of a personality, she looked lovelier than ever with her auburn hair cut pageboy style.

They found Peggy Fox incoherent and whimpering in pain. Before they left, Simon insisted on seeing her consultant and was told the cancer had reached her kidneys. All hope was gone: she might live for two years or two months.

They walked the two miles back to the city centre in pouring rain, letting buses pass, unable to face strangers; sobbing and smoking and damning the unfairness of it all; calling at an off-licence for half a bottle of rum and gulping greedily from it, partly to erase the pain, partly to mask their dread at returning home with the news.

Simon had held back the tears throughout his mother's illness, confident that he could withstand the ordeal ahead. He had done it when his father died. But what of his widowed grandfather? Fred Bains had lived with them almost constantly during his daughter's spells in hospital, helping to keep the house in order and get the kids off to school.

Simon's voice cracked as he turned to Lynne and asked, 'How do you tell someone their only child is dying?'

Worst still, what of his sister and brother, Dawn and Paul, just 14 and 16 and soon to be orphans?

He was just 22 and felt little more than a child himself at times. But he would have to be their rock. There was no one else. The alternative – to let what remained of his family fall apart – was a prospect so horrifying he could barely articulate it.

7

MAURICE Goodacre worshipped his cousin, a few months his senior.

They grew up three doors apart, amid the boom and clatter of blast furnaces in full flow, in soot-caked terrace streets built to house the families of men who had escaped the dole queues of the north-east for jobs at Tyler's Steelworks.

The boys were never without food but toys were few and their fathers arrived home too weary from work and the gallon of ale at the Foundryman's Arms that habitually followed, to play with them.

Maurice and Colin became constant playmates, filling their days with football and marbles; train-spotting from Dovethorpe Bridge, where they hung their heads in singeing steam as wondrous locos passed below.

They ranged rubble heaps and wriggled through abandoned pipes and played knights and dragons, cowboys and Indians, gladiators and explorers. They door-knocked and roly-polyed, climbed trees and raided birds' nests and walked miles on picnics of ketchup sandwiches and bottles of sugared water, always, it seemed, on glorious sunny days that ended with the giggling, panting pair of them lying flat out, staring at the sky and dreaming of spaceships and aliens.

When Colin passed his 11-plus and headed for grammar school, leaving his cousin consigned to the brutal regime of a secondary modern, Maurice had nothing but pride. And when Colin was taken on by the *Bugle* as a trainee reporter, his cousin dug deep into the modest savings of a general labourer to throw a party.

Maurice was one of life's plodders. He would never be wealthy but considered himself a rich man, for who needed money when you had a roof over your head, enough to get by and a wife and daughter whose love and laughter made the sun shine every day?

Neither of his loved ones had an inkling of his misery at work since a brash and burly figure had joined the same gang of labourers.

Maurice went about his job quietly, diligently, but never in a hurry and the wisecracking Ron Castle soon showed himself the archetypal bully, nicknaming him 'Lightning' and engineering a series of practical jokes.

One day, Maurice discovered a snail in his lunchbox; another, a stink bomb in the well of his car. When a klaxon sounded inches from his ear one lunch break, he shrieked and threw his mug of tea into the air.

The final indignity awaited him in the gang's grubby toilet cubicle. Desperate to relieve himself, Maurice was soon sitting in urine and excrement. Someone had covered the bowl with a tight and near-invisible layer of clingfilm.

The laughter and jeers as he stumbled out, wet and stinking, trousers around his ankles, plagued his fitful sleep that night, and when the alarm clock sounded next day, he turned over, ignoring wife Brenda's pleas to get up for work. The following day was the same, and the next. He could not bear the thought of facing that pack of hyenas and no amount of telling him to pull himself together would change his mind.

But no work meant no pay and even the normally unflappable Brenda began to worry about rent and bills. It was only when she threatened to call in Colin that Maurice turned to his GP for a course of antidepressants.

His insomnia went away but, in the dull haze that enveloped his waking hours, he found himself one Saturday morning being manhandled by a store detective as he bypassed the tills and walked out of the Co-op with a pack of mince.

He did not even like mince.

Arrested and told he would be reported for prosecution, he turned to the one person he knew with any clout and begged for help.

He dared not tell Brenda. And he swore to his cousin that if it got into the paper that he was a shoplifter, he would end his life.

How many times had Colin heard that cry? How often had he asked would-be reporters, 'If your own brother was taken to court, could you cover the story?'

It was one of his golden rules: no favours, not for anyone.

But, as he looked at his once-proud cousin weeping before him, all his high ideals seemed no more than hot air.

'No promises,' he said, 'but I'll see what I can do.'

*

THE editor agonised for three days before making the call. Of all the people to grovel to, it would have to be Jim Richardson. The press had got virtually nothing out of the police since his appointment as head of the town's CID.

He found the inspector surprisingly open to the idea of a chat. To his greater surprise, when they met the next day, the conversation turned to the topic of the new road.

'You know, Mr Goodacre – Colin,' Richardson smiled, 'this wretched saga has gone on far too long, don't you think? And it's having an effect on policing and the morale of the town. Whole areas are derelict, people's pride in the place is sinking, crime's growing. There's a shadow over the whole town. And worst of all, a couple of vulnerable old people are stuck in limbo.

'Now, I'm an adopted son of Brexham, as you know, but I've grown to love the place. I just want what's best for it and I think your newspaper could make a big difference if it got off the fence and told the politicians to pull their fingers out and get the road built.'

As they parted with a handshake, the inspector added, 'Leave that mince business with me. But we're both men of the world, aren't we? Perhaps you could do something for your town in return, eh?'

8

COUNCILLOR Frank Noon left the refreshing chill of Tommy Jepson's living room with a promise to talk once more to the housing department.

Helping the likes of Tommy: that's what being a councillor was all about, not all that rubbish at meetings. Still, Frank understood the council's position. There was no shortage of accommodation across the borough but Tommy was holding out for a specific area. Prospective tenants were for ever trying to dictate where they were housed and officials were loath to set a precedent, especially in a case like Tommy's, where, as yet, they had no legal obligation to do anything.

Silently cursing the return of hay fever, Frank blew his raspberry-cluster nose in a white cotton handkerchief and gave a thoughtful tug of the silvery ponytail that symbolised his defiance of age and conformity. Then he put on the headphones attached to the cassette player in the small rucksack he wore over his shoulders wherever he went and headed for the Black Swan and a lunchtime pint with his favourite reporter.

Frank had promised him a good story but Simon soon found himself under pressure to commit what struck him as an unnatural act: to take up the cudgels for Tommy without writing about it.

'I know it's a good cause,' he said wearily, 'so, give me some quotes and I'll do a story.'

'You're not listening, are you?' Frank's raised voice brought a glance from two old women drinking barley wine at a nearby table. It did no harm to have people thinking he stood up to the press.

'I am listening,' Simon said, 'but if you want a social worker, don't come to me. I report things – that's my job. I've asked Tommy and he won't go on the record. You're the public servant, Frank – do something yourself.'

'I've been trying to, lad, but,' his voice dropped, 'there's some dark forces at work here.'

Simon's eyebrows raised in faint ridicule.

'Someone's trying to drive him out,' Frank continued, 'and if you go putting in the paper that he's a vulnerable pensioner in a wheelchair in a deserted street, who knows what might happen? How would you feel then? Can't you just lean on 'em for me? You know what to do – phone the housing department and tell them you're going to kick up a stink about this frail old man and the heartless bureaucrats who won't give him a new bungalow.'

Simon smiled. 'Sounds like you need a job in journalism.'

'Flatulence'll get you nowhere, sunshine,' Frank chuckled. 'It'd only take you a few minutes and they're not to know you aren't actually going to write 'owt, are they? Just put the wind up 'em and see what happens.'

'And what do I get out of it?'

'Apart from a clear conscience and a good night's sleep?' the councillor grinned. He enjoyed these sparring sessions.

Simon leaned towards him and mouthed, 'Up yours!' Then, loud enough for the barleywine biddies, 'If journalists were half as devious as politicians, we'd never sleep a wink.'

'Here.' Frank rummaged in his carrier bag and slid something under the table. It was a sheet of yellow paper headed with the borough council's crest and three of Simon's favourite words, 'Private and confidential'.

'It's not come from me,' Frank whispered.

'Obviously,' the reporter smiled. 'And I'll do what I can for Tommy, I promise.'

Back at the office, Colin Goodacre was in a bad mood. 'What the hell are we going to splash on this week?' he shouted across the newsroom.

It was two days to press day and the editor liked a front-page fallback in case nothing big broke.

'I might have something,' Simon smiled. 'Give me an hour.'

He re-read Frank Noon's document. Four dustmen had been sacked, it said, after a council officer driving past a remote pub had spotted them drinking outside when they should have been on their rounds.

He phoned Henry Whelan, the dour Tory chairman of the personnel committee, and asked if he'd care to comment.

'I don't know where you've heard that, young man,' said Whelan, 'but you must know that we never discuss personnel matters in public.'

'Well, I know it's true, Councillor Whelan, so we'll be running the story anyway.'

'You do as you see fit,' the chairman said sternly. 'But I will say this: anyone who makes private matters concerning council staff public is a disgrace in my book. They harm the council's efforts to treat its staff with the dignity they deserve and are not acting in the interests of the ratepayer. You can quote me on that.'

Simon replaced the receiver with a smug smile. What might have been two paragraphs would now make 200 words. A call to the dustmen's union would wrap it up. He poked his head around the editor's door and beamed, 'Got a new splash, boss.'

'You should've seen who he's been talking to while you were out,' Gary Bostock said when Simon returned to his desk. 'Only your favourite copper – Detective Inspector "I hate the press" Richardson.'

'Jesus! What about?'

'Daren't ask, mate. Boss's had a face like a slapped arse all day.'

'Believe it or not, he wants to improve press-police relations,' Colin said when Simon tackled him later. 'We just had a chat over a cup of tea but it was a start. God knows we could do with more news from the cops and he says he wants to get some crime prevention messages out there. I told him it'd have to work both ways, though, so we'll see.'

*

THE heaving, grinding, rattling old press shook the premises of J.H. Riddle & Son almost to their foundations as Colin creaked open the back door and climbed the rickety spiral staircase to the press hall.

The antiquated machine was spewing out section two of the week's edition, ready to be paired by hand with section one, since the press could print only eight pages in a run. Sometime before midnight, 10,000 copies in brown-paper bundles of 100 would be loaded on to Transit vans and dropped outside newsagents' shops in time to catch workers on the early shift as they called for snacks and smokes en route to the steelworks.

'Ey up, it's Shagabout! Gonna keep us all friggin' night again?' yelled Lol, the hairy-arsed press manager. 'Get a move on, Colin, we want some ale tonight.'

The editor smiled and raised his right hand in a 'wanker' sign.

'You an' all,' Lol laughed, ''cept I need both hands for mine!'

In the composing room, managing director Dennis Riddle and his nephew Ivor were slotting and squeezing slugs of body type and headline into metal frames in vague imitation of the editor's layouts.

Nothing much changed during Colin's Thursday afternoon visits to the printworks to supervise the final stages of production. There were page proofs to check, the odd ill-fitting headline to reword and coffee to drink while listening to Ivor's exaggerated tales of sexual conquests. But today was different.

He slipped away to the tea room, returning 15 minutes later with several hand-written sheets of copy paper.

'Here,' he handed them to a grumpy-looking man seated at a Linotype machine, 'set that for me, please, Reg.'

With a fascination that never waned, the editor watched as Reg pressed keys that released brass matrices to form lines of type that were quickly cast in lead alloy from a miniature furnace at the back of his huge machine.

'That's the new splash,' he told Ivor. 'Put the sacked dustmen on page five.'

He left two hours later with a heavily inked *Bugle* and an envelope containing unused stories, a small but welcome start to next week's issue.

It had been another triumph of accident over design but there was no elation as he scanned the newspaper's pages, noting the battle-weary advertisement logos and the lifeless pictures that looked like they had been dragged through muddy water.

Investment in the business was desperately needed and half of him yearned for the day the *Bugle*'s elderly owners sold up or passed on.

The other half knew that he might not survive as editor once the paper's century of independence ended with a takeover by a faceless conglomerate.

*

SIMON breezed into the office the next morning, as excited as ever at the prospect of seeing his work in print. At some stage in the next week, two households in every three in the paper's circulation area would be reading what he and the rest of the team had written. Loyal locals had a saying, 'It's not true until it's been in the *Bugle*.'

He grabbed a copy from a bundle in Reception, looked at the front page and gasped. In place of his story about the boozing dustmen, the splash was headed, 'Time to get on with the road!' Below a 'Bugle Comment' byline was an eight-paragraph piece calling on councillors to stop arguing about the project and unite in a campaign for money to get it built.

Not bothering to knock, he walked into the editor's office.

'What the hell's this about, boss?'

'Excuse me, mister!' Colin snapped. 'Who do you think you're talking to?'

This was not the Colin he had grown to admire. They had become more like friends than boss and employee, for ever discussing what stories to cover and how; for ever – until now – agreeing that, at the very least, the road should be put on hold and re-examined to ensure there was no better way to tackle the town's obvious traffic problems.

'Sorry,' Simon sat down with a sigh. 'But what's brought this on? It's a complete about-face. So why the sudden change of heart?'

'It's not really sudden,' Colin said calmly. 'I've been thinking about it for a while. This saga can't go on, you know. Look at the state of the town. We'll be stuck in the bloody dark ages if we don't stop arguing and do something.'

'Fair enough,' said Simon. 'But a bit of warning would've been nice before I discovered I've got to put on a different face when people ask me where we stand.'

'To tell you the truth,' Colin removed his glasses and looked his protege in the eye, 'I wrote that piece at the printer's yesterday – and I enjoyed it. It was like being a reporter again. I just sat and wrote it, using my head instead of my heart, which I probably use too often. I didn't discuss it with you because I knew we'd have an argument. And at the end of the day, buddy, I *am* the editor.'

Simon calmed himself with a visit to Solly's Transport Café and Lodging House. The place was a monument to the days before hygiene regulations but Solly's toasted bacon and fried egg sarnies, wrapped in newspaper, were a gastronomic delight and he devoured one while working through the daily phone calls to the police, fire and ambulance services.

Nothing to report, he set off for the magistrates' court, stopping en route at Annie Shaw's to apologise.

'Dunno how you dare show your face,' she called as he appeared at the back door. 'S'pose yer'd better come in. So, it's true, is it?'

'What do you mean?' The reporter had expected a tongue-lashing but not the uncertainty.

'You know what I mean, mister! Hilda Wright phoned to tell me – 'er as I go to bingo with. So, now that paper of yours thinks the damned road's a good idea? Hmm! And after all them promises! Eeh! I never thought you'd betray us, our own local paper.'

He hung his head. 'I'm sorry, love, but it's nothing to do with me, honestly. I'll explain… but how come Hilda Wright told you? Haven't you seen the paper?'

'None of us 'ave – me, Tommy Jepson. All round 'ere. Nobody's 'ad a paper. Paper lad knocked on t'door just after seven and said 'artshorne's shop were locked up and there were no sign o' Norman. Tommy's phoned Councillor Noon. He knows Norman's brother and thinks 'e'll 'ave a key.'

*

LITTLE had changed in the seven decades in which Norman Hartshorne and his father before him had run a newsagent's and tobacconist's in Pinder Terrace. The red-and-white-striped awning still lolled on rusty supports. The cracked stone floor tiles still said W.D & H.O. Wills. A wire rack stuffed with evening editions and women's magazines still hung from a nail beside the front door.

The tobacco scales had become mere decoration and Marlborough and Gitanes had joined Park Drive and Senior Service on shelves that might have been varnished with their packs in place. The sweet counter's glass front clung to the last flecks of a Cadbury's transfer and Milk Tray bars and Fry's Five Centres stood proudly among the aristocracy of Goodiedom, looking down on the naked proles in their plastic trays – liquorice reels, chocolate mice, jellied bottles, Black Jacks and rainbow drops, shoelaces and fried eggs and great crusted bubble gums sour enough to curl the toes.

Not a square inch of space was wasted. Bats and balls hung in nets from the ceiling and the window was crammed with row upon row of curtain wires dangling kites and baby baths, colouring books and pop guns, sun visors and rain hats, parasols and plasticine, water pistols, combs, cards, chess sets, whistles and toy watches, each with its price written in biro on a rough square of card.

It was Simon's go-to place for smokes and snacks and came with the bonus of a chat with Big Norm, six foot three and 30-odd stone but soft as a pudding.

Norm would smile down from his two chins, his pear-shaped frame squeezed behind the counter, hands resting on a paunch that looked for all the world like a big bass drum, as he told a quick joke that lasted for ever and asked if the ten Park Drive that Simon had just purchased were to take away.

But time, and the road, were catching up with the place. The clearance programme had left few houses within easy walk and no great powers of prophecy were required to know that, before long, Norm would have to bow to the inevitable and sell up.

In the end, it was the fat that got him. Having carted the overnight delivery of *Bugles* and other newspapers inside and locked the door behind him, he keeled over behind the counter. And there he stayed, wedged and dead, until his brother turned up with a key.

The fire brigade had to dismantle the counter to get Norm out.

Simon could have kicked himself for thinking it would make a good story, but it did.

Colin silently wondered if he was partly to blame. Had Norm managed to open one of the bundles and taken ill at the shock of discovering the *Bugle*'s about-turn?

When the news reached Jim Richardson, he rubbed his hands and murmured, 'Another one bites the dust.'

9

LOWERING himself on to a cushion on the floor of his living room, Tommy opened the bottom drawer of his late father's mahogany sideboard and gingerly removed a long, slim bundle wrapped in towelling.

The latest outrage had been the final straw.

The bathroom window had barely been fixed when a dead pigeon appeared, hung by string from the washing line. A week of peace followed and Tommy began to feel settled once more. Then, one evening after steak and kidney pud at Annie's, he returned to find a wave of white paint splashed across the front of his shed.

Attacking the landlord's property was one thing but he was damned if he was going to surrender his beloved workshop to some vandal, whoever they were, whatever their motive.

He told himself that Frank Noon was doing his best to help. He knew that Simon could hardly write a story without his cooperation. And he held out little hope of the police catching the culprit.

So, what was he supposed to do? Sit and wait for the next attack?

He grabbed a bed sheet, a blanket and the towelled bundle from the sideboard and went to his workshop.

The month of June had brought a spate of hot days and warm evenings. Tommy figured he would be comfortable enough sleeping in his workshop, where he could guard his timber creations night and day.

FLICK pushed a note through Tracey's door. In almost childish scrawl it read, 'Tell him Tuesday, 5pm, Hopbrook Lane.'

How he wished he could have knocked and said hello to his daughter.

He had chosen the rendezvous carefully. It was half a mile from home, on a quiet road past a copse where magic mushrooms could be found if one knew where to look: good cover in case he was spotted by anyone he knew. And if they were to see a policeman's car pull up alongside him, he could always say the filth were harassing him.

Richardson was intrigued by the note, but relieved. Too many meetings at the nick might raise suspicion. Besides, a five o'clock finish would make a nice change. He'd pick up a Chinese on the way home, give Eunice a break from cooking. They might watch *The Sweeney* on the box while he tried not to laugh at actors being coppers.

He wrote 'no further action' on the front cover of the file on Colin Goodacre's cousin Maurice and drove to Hopbrook Lane.

Flick checked the road in both directions as the inspector's silver Ford Capri pulled up, then swiftly climbed inside.

'Glad to see you've not got the mutt with you,' said Richardson, promptly driving on. 'Now, what's all this about?'

'This thing wi' the old fella, I don't like it,' Flick scowled. 'Nickin' stuff's one thing. Giving someone a kickin' now and then, sure. But frightenin' some old guy who ain't got no legs – what's that about?'

The officer passed him an envelope. 'You're being looked after well, aren't you?' his voice softer than usual.

Flick counted the notes inside and nodded.

'I'm not paying you to ask questions,' Richardson said. 'Just get the job done and stop pissing around.'

'Why, though?' said Flick. 'What's it to you if the old bloke lives there or moves out? And what happens if I get caught? What am I supposed to say then?'

'Nothing'll happen to you if you just make a nuisance of yourself, then get the hell out. It's not rocket science. Mind you,' the familiar snarl returned, 'if you did get caught, you'd say you were just being a dickhead, wouldn't you? Because if you ever let on about our arrangement, to start with, who's going to believe a thieving toerag like you over a respected member of Her Majesty's Constabulary? And secondly, your old man'd have your bollocks in a blender once I'd had a word with him.'

'Huh! So, I risk gerrin' locked up for summat and I don't even know why I'm doing it?'

'You're better not knowing, believe me. But I'll tell you this: there are some unpleasant people connected with property in this town. Very unpleasant. And the sooner that street's knocked down, the sooner those nice people on the council can get on with tidying up the place, which will be good news for all law-abiding citizens, if not for the likes of you.

'Now,' he said, pulling up half a mile further from Flick's place, 'out you get. The extra walk'll do you good. And don't mess up this time.'

*

TOMMY listened to the eight o'clock news on his transistor radio. It was depressing: public spending cuts on the way; a hammer-wielding maniac killing prostitutes in Yorkshire; fears of water rationing as reservoirs dried up in the heatwave. It was hard to believe this was the same country battered by gales that had killed dozens of people months earlier. No wonder Brits were obsessed with the weather.

A faint glow from the shed's strip light pierced the darkness enveloping the marooned terrace. He turned off his radio and put Count Basie in the cassette player. For the next two hours, the only other sound was that of fine sandpaper on wood.

Suddenly, the alley-side wall began to shake as if kicked or thumped and a voice – a young man's – yelled 'get out of there!'

A pot of varnish fell from a shelf and burst on the workbench.

Tommy heard footsteps running away. Then quiet.

First thing in the morning, he phoned WPC Marshall. She arrived quickly, put a gentle arm around him and promised that she was recording every incident and was determined to catch the culprit. 'I've got a big patch to cover, though,' she frowned, 'so I can only come down here occasionally.'

'Kind words,' Tommy muttered as he waved her goodbye, 'but the truth is, old son, you're on your own.'

It was with trepidation but a new resolve that he returned to the workshop two days later.

He polished off a bottle of Mackeson stout and two slices of buttered fruit loaf, then took hold of the long bundle he had retrieved from the sideboard. Carefully peeling back the strips of brown tape, he unravelled the towelling to reveal an antique sword.

Three feet long, it had seen better days. The steel blade was pitted and rusty but the bronze pommel was elegantly engraved with a crown and the brass guard was embossed with a leaping horse.

God only knew why he had kept it, except that it was his dad's and the stuff of family legend. The old man would fetch it out from time to time to amaze Tommy's pals; otherwise, it had stayed hidden away until Tommy had cleared out his father's effects.

The thought that it might be valuable had crossed his mind but the auction house to which he sent a Polaroid picture said it was worth little more than scrap, so he hid it away again. What else could he do? Carry it across town to the police station? Put it out for the dustmen and risk it falling into the wrong hands?

He resolved to clean it up and found some wire wool and a tube of metal polish in a drawer. Eventually it began to gleam.

He held the sword aloft and pointed it towards the door. If anyone tried to enter his sanctum, perhaps that would make them think twice.

10

SIMON was thinking about his name. He needed something, anything, to take his mind off the reality.

Fox. It was quite ridiculous. As a child, he had vowed to change it as soon as he could. No memory of school days was more vivid or painful than the teasing he endured at the hands of other children, who liked nothing more than a surname they could apply to some other creature or object.

As the years passed, he found himself wondering if people were shaped to some extent by their surnames. Had his own given him the cunning required for a career in journalism? Did the Planks grow up to make furniture and the Hobbs to make kettles? Were all the Pratts idiots?

The cortege made its way along streets where people no longer stood in silence and raised their hats to the dead. It crunched up the gravel driveway of the crematorium, past saplings that never seemed to grow on clean-shaven turf sprouting bowls of memorial posies.

Simon gripped their hands in turn – Paul, Dawn, his grandad, Lynne – and gave them a gentle smile that said: We're OK, we can make it, just hang on.

Two years or two months, the consultant had said. Peggy Fox had lasted seven weeks.

Simon had scratched for comfort in the knowledge that she had not lingered in pain. But guilt clung to him like a sea fog.

Mother and son had talked about euthanasia, in the abstract. They would say that if one ever faced a slow and painful death, the other would pass the tablets, but when it came to the crunch, he had lacked the courage to tell her she was dying. How could he? How could he tear away the last shreds of hope?

Had he deluded himself? His mother was no fool. She must have known the reality. Didn't everyone know when their time had come? Or had she been waiting for him to tell her the most momentous thing he could ever utter, the one truth she had a right to know?

Peggy's coffin was being carried inside.

Five years and 226 days had passed since he last visited this awful place.

Ex-Royal Navy signalmen George Fox was a man of ready wit and charm, strict at times but barrels of fun. In the months before his death, father and son had forged an adult friendship. At 16, the bud of Simon's childish mind had begun to blossom and George relished the intellectual challenge. In long and heated debates, they set the world to rights and even swapped tastes in women.

In his dad's one-man barber's shop, Simon earned pocket money by sweeping up snips of hair and occasionally answering a rap on the off-sales window to sheepish men of 20 or 60 (they all looked old in their overcoats and flat caps) who asked to see his father, then hurried off with their pack of three.

The coffin was being placed on the conveyor.

Simon told himself he should be focusing on the moment. But it was too hideous.

Instead, he pictured the blue and white pom pom hat his father wore on the last day of his life as he set off to Hull to do some work for the in-laws. Two hours later, grief made its debut in Simon's life. George Fox had lifted the handles of a wheelbarrow full of concrete and dropped dead from a heart attack.

Simon last saw him at the chapel of rest as his mother screamed disbelievingly at a stiff, cold lump of flesh in a padded box. It looked in need of a shave and reminded him of someone he once knew.

Less than six years had passed and yet he struggled to remember his father's face, the feel of him, his voice, his smell.

He could not have imagined that life could go on without him, yet George had taught him as much in death as in life. From the moment he saw him dressed for his funeral, Simon vowed to live each day to the full, to value every experience, be it good or bad; to be glad for what he had, rather than mourn its passing.

*

THAT evening, WPC Wendy Marshall was true to her word again, patrolling Pinder Terrace as her afternoon shift came to an end.

She shone her torch along the lonely road and the back alley with its solitary street light but found nothing to raise suspicion.

She was relieved to see Tommy's house and garden in darkness. At least he was not drawing attention to himself by working late in that shed of his.

She had just left the alley to begin her walk back to the station when she heard a shriek, followed by thudding footsteps and a shape stumbling out of the darkness.

11

SIMON and Lynne had booked the day after the funeral as holiday, to start sorting things out at home, as they'd put it, though neither was sure what that would entail or where to begin.

Peggy had languished in hospital for three months and, though they knew she would never be coming home, the reality now hit them.

Grandad Bains had all but moved in but he had a life of his own back in Yorkshire and announced that he would be going home at the weekend. It pricked his protective instincts but it was for their own good: they would have to cope on their own sooner or later.

The couple's day off had hardly begun when the phone in the long, draughty hall rang and Dawn raced to answer it. 'Simon,' she called, 'it's a Mrs Shaw and she sounds upset.'

He took the receiver, returning shortly with a look of disbelief. 'It's old Mr Jepson,' he said. 'He's been arrested for GBH.'

'Good God! But you're not working today, love, please…?' Lynne scowled.

'Sorry, babe, but he's in court this morning. I've got to go in for this. Won't be long. Promise. There's a bus in ten minutes.'

He charged upstairs, tore off his jeans and T-shirt, had a whore's bath, dried roughly, pulled on the white shirt and grey suit he'd worn for the funeral, phoned Colin with the news and reached the bus stop with seconds to spare.

The magistrates' court had two ushers and he was in luck: the helpful one was on duty when he arrived as the 10am sitting was about to start. She guessed why he was there and nodded towards Court 2.

He was surprised to see no one else on the press bench and only two people in the public gallery, a woman and DI Richardson.

Tommy was being wheeled into the dock. He looked ashen as he gave his name, address and date of birth in answer to the court clerk.

'You are charged,' the clerk said, 'with wounding with intent to cause grievous bodily harm to Edward Thacker.'

Who the hell was Edward Thacker, Simon wondered. And what had he got to do with Tommy?

The resident police solicitor, a tall, hard-faced man named Watts, was about to tax the reporter's shorthand skills with his familiar rapid delivery. 'Your worships,' he said, 'the allegation is that the defendant stabbed Mr Thacker with a sword at an outbuilding at the defendant's property in Pinder Terrace.

'The defendant was arrested only last night and the injured party is currently under observation in hospital. As your worships will appreciate, this charge can only be heard before a crown court and I would therefore ask for a remand in custody for seven days.'

There was a gasp from the gallery.

'Mr Ingles?' Arthur Pemberton, the headmasterly chairman of the bench, peered at the wiry figure of duty solicitor Bob Ingles, renowned for his passionate defence of no-hopers.

'Your worships, there is no dispute that the injury was caused by my client,' said Ingles. 'However, he was acting in self-defence of his property and his person. He intends to plead not guilty and is confident that a jury will acquit him.

'Mr Jepson is a respectable gentleman of 72 years who has never been in trouble before. He is severely disabled and unlikely to abscond. I respectfully submit that to send him into custody today would cause undue hardship.'

'Mr Watts?' said the chairman.

'Your worships,' said the prosecutor, 'the police have serious concerns about the accused returning to his home address, where the offence took place, given its isolated nature and the risk that publication of his address in the newspapers might expose his vulnerability to criminal types.'

'Hmm,' Pemberton stroked his chin. 'So, what can you offer us, Mr Ingles?'

'I would ask your worships to grant bail, subject to Mr Jepson residing with his daughter, who is in court today and willing to stand surety.'

'Very well, let us hear from her.'

The lawyer motioned to the gallery and a stout, middle-aged woman with a snub nose and a loose perm entered the witness box.

'Are you Mrs Jean Palethorpe, of Eddison Square, Darley Estate?' asked Ingles.

'That's right.'

'And are you the daughter of the gentleman in the dock, Mr Thomas Jepson?'

'I'm tempted to say "unfortunately" but…'

'Just answer the question, please, Mrs Palethorpe,' the chairman smiled.

'Sorry, your lordship. Yes, I'm his daughter, his only child.'

'And would you,' said Ingles, 'be willing to have him live with you pending his trial and make sure that he is of good behaviour?'

'He'd better be or I'd neck him…'

The chairman frowned.

'Sorry, your lordship! It's just that it's a big shock, coming to court to vouch for your dad. Nothing like this has ever happened to our family.'

'Quite,' said Ingles. 'And I understand from our conversation today that you would be willing to stand surety for him in the sum of £500.'

She nodded.

'Are you quite clear what that means?' asked Pemberton. 'That if he fails to obey the rules of his bail in any way, you could lose £500?'

'I understand. And I know he'd never let that happen to me. But,' her voice cracked, 'please don't send him to prison.'

'Mr Watts?' said the chairman.

'Your worships, the prosecution is happy with the conditions outlined but would also ask that the defendant is ordered not to communicate with the injured party pending his trial at the crown court and to observe a curfew between 7pm and 7am.'

'Mr Jepson,' said the chairman, 'are you willing to abide by all of those conditions?'

'Yes sir.'

'Very well. You are released on bail pending committal to the crown court.'

Tommy nodded and, as his daughter wheeled him out of the courtroom, he felt like cheering and crying at the same time.

'Tommy!' Simon hissed as he hurried after them, 'Can I have a word?'

'Sorry, owd son, but my lawyer says I'm to say nowt to t'press, and I reckon it's best if I do as I'm told.'

The reporter was crestfallen. He knew only too well that the contempt of court laws meant that very little of the case could be reported before it went before a jury, which could be months or even a year ahead. But he had hoped to get some background from Tommy, something to give the *Bugle* an edge when the trial took place, at which point the national press would be all over it. 'Legless man defends home against intruder.' It was a story with universal appeal.

*

DI Richardson had mixed feelings about Edward Thacker's surprise appearance in the saga of 12 Pinder Street: anger at Flick's failure to finish the job, but relief that the attack could not be linked to previous events.

Whether he believed a convicted burglar's claim that he was innocently taking a leak against a garden shed when an old man stuck a sword into his arm was another matter. The fact remained that serious injury had been inflicted with a deadly weapon.

Had things gone to plan, Tommy would have decided enough was enough and moved out of his own accord. As it was, he could hardly be evicted now. Innocent until proven guilty, and all that.

Still, Thacker's intervention might achieve the desired result in the long run. The inspector would just have to bide his time.

He called Divisional HQ straight after the court hearing. 'There'll be a lot of press interest,' the assistant chief constable warned. 'Make sure we do this absolutely right.'

Thanks for teaching granny to suck eggs, Richardson muttered as he put the phone down.

He summoned Wendy Marshall, checked that her notes of the night's events tallied with her statement and told her to visit Thacker as soon as possible to double-check his story.

Eunice Richardson was close to tears when she heard the news. 'I can't believe it, Jim,' she said. 'I know I never met Mr Jepson but from what I heard, he was just a nice old man who kept himself to himself. What can have got into him?'

'Well,' her husband soothed, 'I know he'd had some vandalism and perhaps he got a bit paranoid, living alone in what's basically a demolition site. You know how old folks can go a bit doolally.'

'Mmm. It's so sad, though. Well, we'll have to keep the house on for him, until this business is sorted out.'

'Of course,' he said, hugging her close. 'First thing's first, let's get the place secured. Give Mr Tooms a ring, love, and ask him to board the place up. I think legally we'll have to keep charging Tommy rent to safeguard his tenancy but tell Tooms to knock it down to a couple of quid a week, eh?'

'Good idea, darling,' Eunice smiled. 'Bless you.'

*

SATURDAY brought more dawn-to-dusk sunshine in Britain's hottest summer on record and even in his thinnest jeans and T-shirt, Richardson was sweltering as he left the house shortly before midday.

Eunice's elderly mother had come to stay and the two of them were enjoying a day in the garden. The inspector was on undercover work for the regional crime squad.

Or so he said.

Tracey slipped a note, starting time and place, through the half-open window of Flick's caravan and delivered Lucy to expectant babysitters.

Mum was in her blue housecoat, making bacon butties. Dad was in his tracksuit bottoms and an AC/DC T-shirt that strained against his large paunch. He was clearing space at the kitchen table and had a Sooty and Sweep jigsaw awaiting his granddaughter's attention but Lucy ran straight to her Auntie Sharon, winding her with a leap into her midriff and squealing, 'Let's play dressing-up!'

Tracey ruffled her kid sister's hair, gave her dad's bald head a pat, kissed her mum on the cheek and left with a shout of 'thanks again, back about five'.

She had told them she was meeting an old school friend for a Wimpy and a few drinks. Her dad had huffed that she had a man on the go, and she had laughed it off, dreading to think what he would say if he knew she was having an affair with a married man, and a copper at that.

She silently cursed Jim for making her walk so far but knew it made sense to take precautions. Her family was notorious as it was and she could feel eyes all over her as she passed neighbours who spent much of the year in stone-faced isolation but now laughed and chatted over garden fences, transformed by the magic of a few weeks of sunshine.

The inspector watched her approach in his rear-view mirror. She looked ravishing in white cheesecloth blouse and skimpy pink skirt.

'Damned ladybirds!' she said, brushing at her top as she climbed in beside him.

'Swarms of them all over the country, apparently,' he laughed. 'Just heard it on the radio. They're so desperate for hydration they're drinking people's sweat.'

'Urgh!' she shuddered. 'God, I love the sun, Jim, but when's this crazy summer going to end?'

He leaned over to kiss her and asked if she had remembered the note. 'Of course,' she tutted. 'You know, Jim, I'm impressed – and a bit freaked out – at how you've got my big brother on the straight and narrow.'

'I wouldn't go that far, sweetheart. But he's done all right for me. That's strictly between us, of course. You know what some of the nutters round here would do if...'

'Wotchya take me for?' she pouted and they laughed as the car pulled away.

A new shopping precinct had opened in Wetherston and they explored it hand in hand, anonymous, enjoying the freedom to act like a normal couple for once.

He bought her some shoes and a peaked cap from Chelsea Girl. They called at Boots for a bottle of Charlie, her favourite perfume, and she screwed her nose up as he added some Blue Grass for Eunice.

Steak and chips and trifle were washed down with a bottle of Blue Nun at the city's noted Berni Inn and he parked in a secluded layby on the way home, where the danger of being caught only added to the thrill of sex on the back seat.

He dropped her off where they had met and was in good time for his meeting with her brother.

*

EVENTS of the past week had convinced Flick there was such a thing as fate after all. Eddie Thacker's arrest meant he would be out of the inspector's pocket, even if the cash had come in handy.

'Suppose you've seen the local rag?' Richardson said.

Flick smirked.

'Seems you're a lucky lad. Could've been you that got a sword in his arm.'

'Me lucky?' said Flick. 'You ain't done so bad yersen, 'ave yer? Kept yer 'ands clean and looks like yer got what yer were after.'

'So, how come young Thacker got there first? And do I get a refund now?'

'Ha bloody ha! I were gonna go back next day. Didn't want to risk it too soon after I'd given the old fella a fright. Thought I might take a box of matches with me next time.' Flick bared his missing front teeth in a menacing smile. 'Then that twat Thacker did us both a favour.'

'You know him then?'

'Only from knockin' around town. But get this – turns out I were in the Unicorn the night it 'appened. He came in and sat wi' some other lads and I left soon after.'

'So, he's not seen you around Pinder Terrace, not asked you about the place?'

'Fuck no! I 'adn't seen him for yonks.'

'OK. Just keep your nose clean. And not a word to anyone. Or else.'

'Yeah, I know. See yer around, copper.'

12

HARRY Prendergast had put off the task he was about to perform for as long as he dared without risking a reprimand from his boss.

The cheerful welfare officer from the War Pensions Department had taken a shine to what he privately called the Fox colony, having visited several times during Peggy's illness to check how her 'cubs' were getting on. The long hair would have put him off Simon from a distance but Prendergast concluded that he was a sensible lad and the youngsters were clean and courteous.

When he turned up again five days after the funeral, Paul and Dawn were watching cartoons on TV but slipped effortlessly into homework mode and even prepared tea and biscuits while their visitor small-talked with the grown-ups and steeled himself for a question that never came easy.

'Right,' he said. 'I have two things to tell you, one of them good and one – well, we'll have to see about the second.'

'OK,' Simon frowned. 'Let's have the good news first.'

'It's only a crumb of comfort, I'm afraid, but as you know, your mother received a war widow's pension and the younger children now qualify for a small allowance towards their upkeep.'

'That's good. And the other thing?'

'Well, have you thought about who'll look after Paul and Dawn?'

'What do you mean?' Simon bristled. 'They'll stop here, of course.'

'Well, I'd like to see that, too, but...'

'But what?'

'The thing is, legally speaking, now that your mother's not here, someone has to decide who has custody of them. As they're under 16, they're technically orphans, which means they're the responsibility of the State.'

'Put them in care, you mean? No way!'

'Steady on,' Prendergast smiled. 'I've not said anything about that but there does have to be a legal guardian. Now, as you know, because your father's heart condition was linked to his navy service, Paul and Dawn come under the War Pensions Board. I suspect that if they were at the mercy of Social Services... well, one hates to think what might happen. So, am I to take it that you'd be willing to be the children's guardians?'

'Definitely,' said Simon and Lynne as one.

'And how would the children feel about that?' said Prendergast.

'We want to stay with them,' gushed Dawn, nudging a nod from Paul, who had drifted back into *Tom and Jerry*.

'Good! Then let's get some forms filled in and I'll give your application my blessing, although I have to tell you it's the board that has the final say.'

'You can't see any problems, though?' Simon frowned.

'No, I don't think so. The only thing is,' Prendergast stroked his military moustache for reassurance, 'the board is rather keen that guardianship goes to married couples.'

The four looked at each other in mock horror. 'Well then, Si,' Lynne grimaced, 'you'd better make an honest woman of me.'

13

FRANK Noon clocked off from his morning shift at Tyler's Steelworks, walked briskly home, washed, changed and headed for a lunchtime drink with Tommy Jepson.

The councillor had news about Annie and wondered how the old boy was bearing up as his trial loomed, after two months on bail.

He stopped en route for a swift one at the Dog and Partridge. It turned into a leisurely two as he chatted to a few old-timers taking a break from their allotments by playing dominoes and smoking marijuana, bold as brass, with two young scallies who had evidently spent the morning poaching.

He left with a carrier bag containing a cabbage, half a dozen eggs and a rabbit, but had declined the spliff: last time he had smoked that stuff, he and Simon ended up playing hide and seek in the cemetery, whispering and giggling in the dead of night until Simon, attempting to climb the perimeter railings, caught his jeans on a spike and ended up wailing for help as he dangled upside-down over 'Ezekiel Britton, Called To Higher Service'.

Frank could picture the headline if the Tories had found out: RED FRANK IN DRUG-CRAZED GRAVEYARD RAMPAGE.

It was Friday, the *Bugle* was out and, for a few hours, the pressure to produce stories was off, so when Frank appeared at the newsroom window and mouthed 'get your coat', Simon jumped at the chance to take a break from rewriting press releases.

'So, what's all this about?' he asked on the bus to Darley Estate.

'I want to see Tommy,' Frank said. 'Thought we'd take the old lad out for a pint. And I've got something to tell him.'

Tommy was ready and waiting at Jean's gate and they took turns to push him to the Half Moon.

'How you getting on then, Tom?' Simon asked, returning from the bar with three pints of Guinness – 'on expenses' he lied, as if his MD would sanction such extravagance.

'Not bad at all, my owd,' Tommy smiled. 'Jean's done me proud. Set me a bed up in t'front room, she 'as, and I get a cooked breakfast most mornings.'

'Bloody 'ell,' said Frank, 'you've landed on your feet. Think I ought to try stabbing some thieving toerag.'

'Plenty of candidates at the town hall, Frank,' Simon laughed. 'You've not been back then, Tom? To your place?'

'Nah. Can't really – it's boarded up to stop it bein' wrecked. Our Jean 'ad a word wi t'landlord. He's keeping mi tenancy on for a "minimal rent" as she put it. She's a good lass.'

'I was up your street yesterday, as it happens,' said Frank. 'Got some good news for your Annie.'

'She ain't *my* Annie,' Tommy laughed, 'though it ain't for want o' tryin'. Anyway, what's up?'

'Council's found her a flat. Only about half a mile away. Smart little place at Bromley Terrace.'

'I know it,' Tommy smiled. 'Be ideal for 'er, that would. Close to t'shops and t'bus goes by regular. And what's she 'ad to say?'

'She's dead chuffed,' said Frank. 'Triumphant, you might say. Always said she'd only go somewhere that suited her and that's what she's got. But...'

'But what?'

'Well, she's worried about leaving you. I think she misses having you nearby. But you know what she's like – won't admit it.'

'I bloody do,' Tommy chuckled. 'Stubborn beggar is that one.'

'Says you'd struggle to cope without having her nearby.'

'Aye, well, she might not 'ave me nearby much longer.'

'How's that?'

'I dunna think I'll be going back there, not now. Someone wants me out and look where it's got me.'

'You're damned right,' said Frank. 'I try raising it in council meetings but I get slapped down. It's nowt to do with our council, they say, it's a county matter. Some of this,' he stooped to pull up a trouser leg, 'if you ask me.'

'You've done all you can, Frank, and I'm grateful. But I canna carry on as I've bin doin'. They've won, whoever they are, and anyroad, I might have a new place soon, courtesy of Her Majesty.'

'They won't send you down,' Simon huffed.

'Well, we'll soon see, son. Solicitor came round yesterday – got a rough court date in a couple o' months' time, late October. Pretty quick, according to t'solicitor. Reckons it's a straightforward case. I could get owt from five years to life, wi' what they've charged me wi', though he reckons I stand a good chance o' gerrin off. But he would, wouldn't he?'

'Talkin' o' which, I 'ear you're getting' a life sentence, Simon.'

'Yeah, two weeks tomorrow we'll be married with children.'

'She's a brave lass!' Tommy chuckled. 'And from what I've seen, yer punchin' above yer weight, lad. Good on yer!'

'She's a diamond, Tom. And you know we'd love to see you there.'

'Aye, well, I'm keepin' a low profile, till t'trial. Anyroad, if I get off, we'll get pissed together, eh? But first thing I'll do is put in for a council place, anywhere in town, as long as it's ground floor and there's room for mi workshop. As Jean says, she's gorra car and can pop an' see me anytime. Fresh start might do us good. As for Annie, bless 'er, tell her from me that she's to take what they're offerin' – and be sure she gets top whack for 'er place.'

They left him at Jean's gate, two pints and a whisky chaser to the good and looking forward to *Crown Court* on the telly – 'to get me in practice', he winked.

'Didn't see that coming, about Annie,' Simon said on the bus back. 'Looks like the end of the road for Pinder Terrace, what with Big Norm gone and Annie getting a new place. I'll have to call round and do a story on her. Quite a victory, that. And I presume you wouldn't be averse to giving a comment for publication, Councillor Noon?'

Frank smiled.

'Another blow for the anti-road lobby, though.'

'No thanks to your paper,' Frank snorted.

'That was as big a shock to me as anyone, you know.'

'I know that, lad. You can't help it if your editor's been got at.'

'You reckon?' Simon looked askance. He still regarded his editor as a man of principle, annoyingly so at times.

'I do reckon. But that road's not guaranteed, not by a long chalk. They've still got to find the money for it and there's the elections next year, so with a bit of luck our lot'll be in charge here and at County Hall. Then we can bury the damned thing for good.'

14

THE wedding of Simon George Fox and Lynne Elizabeth Palmer was done and dusted within eight weeks of Prendergast's ultimatum.

They had talked before about marriage, ruling it neither in nor out. Forced to face the prospect, they saw it as one more thing that had to be done; another challenge to rise to. Despite everything, life was a glass half full.

Simon would have settled for a register office. He hated the bowing and scraping to a god apparently so superior that mere mortals knew what he thought and dared not write his name without a capital 'H' in case He took offence. And if He did exist, Simon hated Him for what He had done to his family.

Lynne had hoped to marry in the church where she was christened, confirmed, said Mass and went to Confession. She won without an argument but abandoned the idea with a snort of derision when the Catholic priest said she would have to sign an oath to do all she could to raise their children in the faith, regardless of her husband's views.

The Church of England had no such qualms. The vicar gladly took their money and rushed through the reading of the banns.

Dawn and Lynne's big sister, Sandra, joined the bride-to-be on a marathon tour of city shops until they ended up back where they had started and settled for floral numbers, off the shelf, from Debenhams.

There were cars, choristers, bellringers', flowers, food and invitations to organise but helping hands in abundance. A phone call from Tommy was enough to ensure free use of the miners' welfare for the reception. Lynne's mum's pub darts team promised to do the catering but, with two days to the wedding, a national strike by bakery workers sent a posse of uncles on a tour of village shops in search of bread and sausage rolls to feed 100.

The countdown to 3pm arrived with a jangle of nerves and queues for the toilets.

Lynne's dad was puffed up with pride as he led his little girl to the altar.

Teetering on a pair of silver platform shoes, Simon was struck so violently by nerves at the altar that his trouser legs flapped.

Paul, fidgety in his maiden suit, did his big brother proud as best man and it was only after he had puked on the stairs that the real reason he had offered to collect leftover drinks became clear.

Napkins dabbed at watery eyes as Simon proposed a toast to 'absent friends' but an unwritten rule was almost universally obeyed: this was a day to be merry.

Peggy would have wanted it that way.

Grandad Bains endured the throbbing disco with the same resilience with which, for the children's sake, he had masked the months of misery and, when the party at last drew to a close, even the bride and groom's weekend-hippy friends, done up in best T-shirts and knee-high boots and reeking of patchouli oil, emerged from the marijuana haze of their table in a dark corner to join aunts and uncles, tots and teenagers in a frenzied Hokey Cokey on the dancefloor.

*

HOME life soon settled into something resembling a routine for Simon, Lynne and 'the kids' not much younger than themselves.

Dawn relished the new bohemian atmosphere of the family home. Her parents' landscape paintings and old-fashioned armchairs gave way to pop posters and floor cushions and a succession of Simon and Lynne's pals turned up with psychedelic LPs and pouches of strange tobacco.

Life seemed wild and exciting and Dawn's grief was veiled by a newfound popularity at school as classmates vied for a sleepover.

Lynne helped her through the trauma of periods and acne and was always there for her, gently guiding but never judging.

Paul had a chin full of bumfluff and a voice that alternated between growl and squeak. He also had a girlfriend and what remained of his spare time was devoted to football. He had his grandfather's build and at, six feet, was already two inches taller than his stand-in dad. As a centre-half with Brexham Town Juniors, he showed an assuredness on the ball and a bite in the tackle that left Simon, for ever cheering him on from the sidelines, thinking his kid brother could go far.

Peggy had not made a will, so probate was not straightforward, with three children to inherit but two unable to receive their share until they were 18. Whether it had to be quite so complicated was something Simon seriously doubted while making numerous taxi trips to see a solicitor who appeared to charge by the full stop but the fledgling family's money pressures were eased by the £600 Peggy had secreted in jars of coins and bundles of notes in drawers and wardrobes. For a rainy day.

Lynne changed her hours at the building society to suit the kids' school times and found new skills and reserves of energy to cope with the task of running a home. So comfortably did she assume the role of mother and confidant that outsiders found it hard to believe she was not born to it.

15

GEORGIO'S Café, on Brexham High Street, was renowned almost as much as a hotbed of gossip as for its Greek owner's coffee, made with hot milk and dusted with cocoa powder, and his early-morning regulars were animated by a snippet on the nine o'clock local radio news.

It was the opening day of Tommy Jepson's trial and the accused was at that moment being briefed by his solicitor at Westerton Crown Court, having travelled the six miles in a wheelchair-friendly taxi with an equally friendly reporter.

'Poor bugger,' rasped a cloth-capped figure through coffee foam. 'Fancy taking an old chap like that to court!'

'Mrs Shaw – yer know, little Annie – were in t'hairdresser's yesterday,' said a middle-aged blonde with black roots. 'She were telling us what he's 'ad to put up wi'.'

'I tell you something,' Georgios shouted above the hiss of the coffee machine, 'I'd give that boy more than a jab in the arm. Give me that sword and I cut his bloody 'ead off!'

*

JEAN reached for Annie's hand as they climbed the steps to the entrance to Shire Hall, glancing at Justice with her scales and sword above the arched doorway. Something resembling justice had been dispensed behind the walls of this grey stone edifice for 200 years.

'Bloody 'ell! Where now?' Jean frowned as they stepped into the cavernous, marbled foyer, its walls adorned with coats of arms and gilt-framed paintings of lords and ladies.

'Ooh, dunna whittle!' said Annie and off she set in search of a man in a gown. Amused by this little woman with her broad dialect, the usher led them to the public gallery, where they squeezed on to a bench just as a voice below boomed, 'All rise! All manner of persons having anything to do before Her Majesty's crown court judge, draw near and give your attendance.'

In the oak-panelled splendour of Number One Court, serried ranks of barristers, instructing solicitors, instructing solicitors' clerks, social workers and probation officers stopped whispering and shuffling papers and bowed as a thin-faced man in a purple and black gown settled in his carved throne.

The *Bugle* team had had reason to be cheerful even before the trial began. Scheduled to start on a Tuesday, it had been put back a day when another case overran. Now, rival media would be only a day ahead before the local rag hit the streets on Friday with the story all Brexham would be talking about.

There was another bonus: the trial was before the highly quotable Judge Alexander 'Sandy' Widdowson, Recorder of Wetherston, known for his withering put-downs of ill-prepared lawyers.

Annie and Jean looked down from the crowded gallery as Tommy, dapper in black blazer and pink shirt, with red National Union of Mineworkers tie, pushed himself up by his elbows in a dock surrounded by spiked railings, where sheep thieves had once been sentenced to hang.

Simon had seen the prosecutor in action before. Gerald Dessaur was a stern man of little humour. Tommy's brief, however, was an unknown quantity, a QC from Birmingham by the name of James Matthews.

On the press bench the man from the *Bugle* was flanked by a middle-aged hack from the *Daily Mirror* and an earnest young woman from the Press Association, whose reports would feed newsrooms up and down the land as the trial progressed.

The journalists' pens hovered over clean pages in spiral notebooks on a desk carved with the names of their predecessors in moments of boredom, as the court clerk asked, 'Are you Thomas Elijah Jepson?'

Simon imagined Annie stifling a titter at the mention of Tommy's secret middle name.

'I am,' Tommy said sternly.

'You are charged with wounding with intent to cause grievous bodily harm to Edward Thacker, contrary to Section 20 of the Offences Against the Person Act 1861. How do you plead, guilty or not guilty?'

'Not guilty.'

'You are further charged with causing grievous bodily harm to Edward Thacker contrary to Section 18 of the Offences Against the Person Act 1861. Are you guilty or not guilty?'

'Not guilty.'

'Please make yourself comfortable, Mr Jepson,' said the judge before turning to the seven men and five women on his right.

'Members of the jury,' he said, 'it will be for you and you alone to deliver a verdict in this case, based on the evidence that you will hear during the course of this trial, and on that evidence alone.

'You should discuss this case among yourselves but with no one else. You must not be influenced by anything you might have read or heard about this case in the media or elsewhere and you must not attempt to obtain further information about it by any means. I trust that is clear.'

The 12 nodded solemnly.

'Eeh, you can 'ear everything up 'ere, Jean.'

It was meant as a whisper but Annie's voice could be heard down below.

Eyebrows raised, the judge looked up at the gallery. 'Members of the public,' he said gently, 'you are most welcome to follow proceedings but please do so in silence.'

Annie shrivelled.

'I'm obliged, Your Honour,' the prosecutor rose. 'Members of the jury,' he said, 'this case is a relatively straightforward one. There is no dispute between the Crown and the defence as regards one crucial element: that the injury to Mr Thacker was caused by a sword which was at that moment in the hands of the accused, Thomas Jepson.

'How and why a very serious injury was inflicted upon Mr Thacker is a matter we will explore in some detail but when you have heard all the evidence, I have no doubt that you will come to the conclusion that the only proper verdict is one of guilty.'

'Thank you, Mr Dessaur,' said the judge. 'Are there any issues you wish to put before the jury at this stage, Mr Matthews?'

'Only this, Your Honour: members of the jury, my client is a 72-year-old severely disabled gentleman of unblemished character who wished only to live in peace in his humble abode and who, having been terrorised by acts of vandalism in the weeks and months preceding the third of June, acted to defend his property and, indeed, his life when Mr Thacker came calling with, we submit, criminal intent.'

That was enough for Mirror Man and PA Girl for now. They shuffled out of the press box, heading for payphones in the foyer to dictate their opening paragraphs to waiting copytakers

'I call my first witness,' said the prosecutor. 'Woman Police Constable Wendy Marshall.'

It was the officer's first crown court trial and her proud parents were in the gallery. She entered the witness box with DI Richardson's words fresh in her mind, 'Don't show any sympathy for nice old Mr Jepson. We all feel sorry for him but remember, he's the accused, not the victim.'

'WPC Marshall,' the prosecutor began. 'Were you on duty in the Pinder Terrace area of Brexham on the evening of Tuesday, June the third, this year?'

'I was.'

'Please tell the court what happened.'

'May I refer to my pocketbook, Your Honour?'

The judge peered over his spectacles. 'When were your notes made, officer?'

'Shortly before midnight, after I got back from the hospital.'

'Very well.'

'Thank you, Your Honour. I was heading back to the station just before my afternoon shift finished at ten o'clock. I'd been along Pinder Terrace and the alley at the back, to check that all was well, and had just left the alley when I heard a shout.'

Mr Dessaur: 'Where did this shout come from, officer?'

'From the direction of Thomas Jepson's garden.'

'What made you think that?'

'Well, I'd visited the house several times in the previous months because Mr Jepson had had some trouble with vandalism.'

'Please continue.'

'I heard footsteps coming towards me. They were fast, like someone running, but I couldn't see anything because it's very dark around there at night. Then, just as I pulled my torch out, this figure appeared.'

'What was it doing, this figure?'

'He was bent over, sort of tumbling. And he seemed to be clutching his right arm. He'd only just appeared when he fell facedown a few feet in front of me.'

'Go on.'

'It was all so quick. I just jumped back. I didn't know what had happened and didn't want to put myself in danger.'

'Very wise,' said the judge. 'Please continue.'

'He was moaning and I could tell he was in pain, so I bent down and asked if he was all right.'

'And what did he say?'

She thumbed through her pocketbook. 'He said "of course I'm not fucking all right, I've been stabbed". Then he took his left hand away from his bare arm – he was wearing a T-shirt – and I could see he was bleeding heavily, so I radioed for back-up and an ambulance. Then I said, "Who stabbed you?" and he nodded back towards the alley and said, "I don't know. I was just leaning against a shed and…"'

'And what, officer?'

'He didn't say any more. He was shivering and I thought he was going into shock, so I told him not to worry and lifted his head off the ground and put my cap under him and covered him with my jacket. I didn't have anything I could use as a tourniquet, so I pressed my palm against the wound and just tried to keep him calm until the ambulance arrived.'

'And how long was that?'

'Seven minutes. It was four minutes before PC 703 Syson arrived. That was 10.08pm. The ambulance arrived three minutes later.'

'I am grateful for your exactitude, officer. What happened then?'

'One of the ambulance staff took over attending to the injured party and applied a tourniquet to the wound. Then, myself and PC Syson walked up the alley to where there was a light shining and…'

'Had you seen a light when you patrolled earlier?'

'No. Everything was dark, apart from a street light a few gardens along.'

'Go on.'

'Well, as we reached what I knew to be the end of Mr Jepson's garden, I could see the light was coming from an outbuilding.'

'This,' said the prosecutor, handing her a large colour photograph, 'is the wooden structure abutting the communal alleyway shown in exhibit eight, is it not?'

'That's correct.'

'Members of the jury, you will see the photograph and a map giving the location of this building on, erm, pages four and five of your evidence bundle. What happened then, officer?'

'As we got nearer, I saw a gentleman I knew to be the defendant.'

'What was he doing?'

'He was sitting inside the doorway of his shed, in his wheelchair and had something in his right hand. I said, "Hello Tommy, are you OK? What's been happening?" And he said "I done him, Wendy. I'd just had enough."'

Dessaur turned to the jury and repeated, '"I done him, Wendy." And what did you take him to mean by that?'

'Objection, Your Honour!' Tommy's barrister leapt to his feet.

Judge Widdowson, 'Yes, Mr Matthews?'

'Your Honour, the officer has not been called as a mindreader. May we stick to the facts and avoid speculation?'

'Objection upheld. Mr Dessaur, perhaps you might frame your question in a different way.'

'I'm obliged, Your Honour. Officer, did the accused say anything else?'

'Yes, he said, "I didn't mean to hurt him. I was just trying to scare him."'

'Go on.'

'Then he threw the thing down that he'd been holding and it made a clanging sound as it hit a slab outside the door. And I said, "OK, just take it easy, we'll sort this out." Then PC Syson read him his rights and told him he was being arrested on suspicion of assault.'

'And did the accused say anything else?'

'He just said, "I'm sorry, Wendy."'

'And did you subsequently examine the object that he'd thrown down?'

'I did.'

The prosecutor reached towards the clerk's bench, 'May I have exhibit one, please?'

'Was this the object, officer?'

Grasping it by the hilt, the barrister held Tommy's sword upright at arm's length and turned to face the witness.

'It looks like it, yes.'

'Had you ever seen this item before, perhaps during your visits to the defendant?'

'No.'

Dessaur turned to the jury. 'It is a fearsome-looking weapon, is it not, ladies and gentlemen? One you might consider to be rather excessive for an elderly gentleman lurking in the darkness of his garden shed with no intention other than to "scare him" as he put it.'

'I must object, Your Honour!' Defence counsel was up again. 'We have heard no evidence of the defendant "lurking".'

'Yes, Mr Matthews,' the judge said wearily. 'Have you finished your examination-in-chief, Mr Dessaur?'

'I have, Your Honour.'

'Very well. Do you wish to cross-examine, Mr Matthews?'

'Briefly, Your Honour, yes. WPC Marshall...' The officer felt her legs wobble and took a deep breath. '...you have told us that my client said he had "had enough of it". Did he say enough of what?'

'No.'

'But did you have any idea what he was referring to.'

'Objection!'

Judge Widdowson: 'Yes, Mr Dessaur.'

'The officer is not here as a mindreader, Your Honour.'

A juror chuckled.

'Quite so,' said the judge. 'Mr Matthews?'

'I'm obliged, Your Honour. Is it true that you had visited the defendant several times in the previous few months, officer?'

'I had, yes.'

'And was this for a cup of tea and a bun? Or something more serious?'

'There had been some vandalism to his property.'

'Rather a lot of vandalism, wouldn't you say? Bricks through windows? Excrement through the letterbox? Paint daubed on the shed? That sort of thing.'

'Your Honour!'

'What now, Mr Dessaur?'

'I hope my learned friend is not suggesting that Mr Thacker had anything to do with these incidents.'

'Not at all, Your Honour,' the defence barrister smiled. 'I am merely trying to paint a picture against which the defendant felt it necessary to tell the police he had "had enough of it".'

'Very well,' said the judge. 'But proceed with caution.'

'I'm obliged. Officer, had Mr Jepson told you, during your previous visits, that he felt someone was trying to frighten him out of his property?'

'That's what he said. I told him I thought it was more likely to be petty vandalism. The street's almost deserted – there's only the defendant's property and one other house occupied because of the clearance programme – so I thought perhaps it was kids messing about.'

'But you reported the matter to your superiors?'

'I logged all the incidents I knew of and told Mr Jepson I'd keep an eye on the area.'

'And how did you do that?'

'I visited several times over the course of six or seven weeks, walking up and down the street and the alleyway, checking that there was no one about.'

'And you saw nothing untoward?'

'That's correct.'

'Thank you, officer. That will be all for now.'

Armpits wet, Wendy Marshall headed for the WRVS tea bar in a corner of the foyer and was ordering a coffee when she felt a tap on her shoulder.

'Let me get this.'

She turned to see a smiling DI Richardson. 'You were great in there, Wendy. Well done.'

*

BACK inside Number One Court the next witness was giving his name and occupation, 'Dr John Crawford, Bachelor of Surgery, employed as a house officer at Norton General Hospital.'

Dessaur: 'Thank you for making time in your busy schedule to attend court today, Dr Crawford. I believe you were on duty on the night of June the third when a young man named Edward Thacker was brought to the hospital.'

'I was indeed.'

'Please tell us what happened.'

'Mr Thacker came in by ambulance and I was alerted by the accident and emergency department. He was in a rather distressed state and had suffered significant blood loss.'

'That was obvious to you immediately?'

'Yes, his right arm was wrapped in a blood-stained cloth and I was informed that a member of the ambulance crew had applied a tourniquet at the scene.'

'Did you then examine him?'

'Not immediately, no. I called a nurse to clean him up and administer analgesic – erm, a morphine injection – to ease the pain. When he'd become calmer, I was able to make a detailed examination of the wound.

'And what were your findings, doctor?'

'The initial incision was a wound to the antecubital fossa – that's a depression to the front of the elbow. There was a penetrating wound, a stab, extending internally by the way the patient had, I suspected, pulled away, partially incising the distal tendon of the biceps brachii' – the doctor pointed, indicating the front of his elbow – 'and then slicing along and down across the brachial artery' – he tipped his index finger so that it moved inward and downward along the arm, dimpling his expensive suit – 'that's the main artery to the arm.'

The reporters swapped frowns; they would have to check spellings with the court clerk later.

'By that I mean,' the doctor continued, 'that the puncture of the skin is small but the wound underneath it is more extensive, longer.'

'A serious injury then?'

'Very serious indeed. It could have resulted in compartment syndrome, which can cause tightness in the muscle and a burning sensation or numbness. Without physiotherapy and regular exercise thereafter, there is a risk of fixed flexion deformity or chronic pain syndrome.'

'But in Mr Thacker's case?'

'I was able to re-attach the nerve and suture the wound. Given a good physiotherapy regime over six to 12 weeks, there is usually minimal deformity.'

'Have you seen Mr Thacker since the surgery?'

'I have and he appears to be recovering well.'

'Thank you, Dr Crawford. Just one more thing: we have heard that first aid was given at the scene. How important might that have been?'

'Extremely important. One can bleed to death within five minutes if a haemorrhage is not stopped. I'd say he was very lucky.'

The prosecutor turned to the jury. 'Lucky to be alive,' he said gravely.

Judge Widdowson: 'Thank you, Mr Dessaur. Do you wish to cross-examine, Mr Matthews?'

'No, Your Honour.'

'Then this seems a good time to break for lunch. We'll resume an hour from now.'

*

'WILL you just look at yourself?'

Mary O'Sullivan's Irish brogue had lost little of its depth in the 20 years since she moved to England with husband Solly to run a transport cafe and lodging house next door to the *Bugle* office. The lodgers tended to be men who had fallen on hard times, and the likes of Eddie Thacker brought out the mum in her.

'What's up wi' me?' he grinned as she placed his porridge on the chequered red and white oilcloth covering one of several tables reserved for lodgers.

'Well now,' she said, folding her arms across her ample bosom, 'where will I start?'

And with that she nipped one shoulder of his treasured Levi's jacket between thumb and forefinger. 'Denim!' she huffed. 'He's going to court in a denim jacket! And what do you call dis t'ing on your chest?'

He looked down at the black T-shirt with its prism logo. 'That's Pink Floyd, Mary,' he said, incredulous. 'Off *Dark Side of the Moon*.'

'Humh! I t'ink de judge'll t'ink *you're* off de Moon when he sees you in dat, dat I do.'

'Don't matter what he thinks, Mary. It ain't me in the dock. I'm the victim, you know, not the bloody criminal. Ooh, sorry!'

'I should t'ink so, Edward T'acker.'

Rough around the edges her clients might be but Mary would have no truck with profanity.

'Now, you listen to your Aunt Mary. I've known a few judges in my time and first impressions count. Dey'll believe you more if you look de part. Our Niall left a few t'ings here when he came over last. You wait here while I have a look upstairs.'

*

MIRROR Man and PA Girl cast envious glances at Simon, sitting in the Shire Hall tea bar with Tommy, Jean and Annie during the lunch break.

They would try to pick his brains later, he suspected, but they'd get nothing out of him: they already had the edge with daily deadlines, not to mention bigger pay packets.

Not that Tommy was giving anything away. 'I'll say all I've got to say in there,' he said between mouthfuls of cheese and onion sandwich.

'Well, don't go breathing on 'em or you'll knock 'em out!' Annie chuckled. Then quietly, 'And try to speak proper when it's your turn.'

'Aw, gi' over, woman!' There was a hint of the old twinkle as Tommy hammed up his beloved dialect. 'They'll tek me as I am and if they dunna believe me, well…'

'Nearly two o'clock,' said. Simon. 'Better go back.'

Inside Number One Court, the prosecutor addressed a thick-set young man with a Rod Stewart mullet. His white shirt was open at the neck beneath a grey suit that looked a size too big.

'Please state your name and occupation for the jury.'

'Edward Thacker,' the witness replied nervously. 'Currently looking for work, Your Honour.'

'Mr Thacker,' the prosecutor began, 'I would like you to tell us exactly what happened on the night of June the third. But first of all, how is the arm?'

'Stiff,' Thacker held it out, crooked. 'Still quite painful but it's getting better.'

'I'm sure we're all delighted to hear you're making progress. Now, what happened? Nice and slowly, please, for the jury.'

'So, I'd come out of the Unicorn…'

'That's a public house on Bamford Road, near to Pinder Terrace, yes?'

'That's right.'

'Were you drunk?'

'Not really. A bit merry. I'd had about four pints. Anyroad, I'd nowt left for bus fare, so I started to walk home and thought I'd go down the alley behind Pinder Terrace cus it's a short cut. I'm walking down there when I suddenly need a slash and I'm looking round for somewhere out of sight when I see an opening next to a shed, so I walk a couple o' yards into t'garden and…'

Dessaur: 'Let me stop you there for a moment, Mr Thacker, so that the jury may get a clear picture. You mentioned an opening. Do you mean a gateway?

'Yeah but there weren't a gate on it.'

'I see. And this gateway was next to a shed?'

'That's right.'

'Had you ever seen this shed before?'

'Can't say I'd noticed it. It were just a shed.'

'And was there a light on? Any indication that someone might be inside?'

'Not then, no, everything were dark. No noise or owt.'

'Please continue.'

'So, I'm up again' the side of this shed – well, I thought it were the side – and I unzip mi jeans and have a slash.'

'Did you make a noise?'

'Only the obvious one' – laughter in the gallery – 'and I think I might have coughed a bit. I'd got a cold.'

'And then?'

'I finished off, then I turned round and leaned against the shed while I got a fag out. Then I lit up and went to go back to the alley but I tripped on summat. I found out later it were a ramp to the shed.'

'What was your reaction?'

'Think I muttered summat like "bollocks!" cus it came keen and it knocked me off balance.'

'And how did you rectify that?'

'You what?'

'You say you were off balance. How did you restore your balance?'

'I fell against the shed.'

'How exactly? With what part of your body?'

'With mi arm, mi right arm. Like this…' He turned to one side to demonstrate.

'And what sort of contact did you make with the shed? Did you brush against it or fall heavily?'

'Pretty heavy cus I were off balance.'

'Was the shed still in darkness at this stage?'

'Yeah.'

'What happened when you fell?'

'I felt summat on mi arm. A dull feeling at first. Then it hit me, the pain.'

'And what was your reaction?'

'I went "aaargh!" and grabbed mi arm. It were wet and I freaked out and just ran but I were clutching mi arm at the same time and I started to fall forward and that's when I saw the copper's torch, just before I fell in front of 'er.'

'You must have been frightened.'

'Objection!' said Matthews. 'Leading the witness.'

Dessaur: 'I'm obliged to my learned friend. Tell us how you felt at this stage, Mr Thacker?'

'Scared. I felt sick, to be honest. I thought I were going to mess meself.'

'Thank you for giving your evidence so clearly, Mr Thacker. That's all for now but my learned friend Mr Matthews might have some questions for you.'

'Indeed I do,' said the defence barrister. 'You've not been entirely truthful with us, Mr Thacker, have you?'

'What d'you mean?'

'Well, you didn't just happen to go there to urinate at all, did you?'

'Yeah, like I said.'

'Isn't the truth that you went there with the intention of burgling the shed?'

'Definitely not!'

'Really, Mr Thacker? But this is your stock-in-trade, is it not? Why, only last year you committed several shed burglaries in the Brexham area and earned yourself six months at Her Majesty's Pleasure.'

The witness looked down.

'In fact, you had been out of prison for only a matter of weeks when you were back to your old tricks.'

'No way! I'm not going back inside. I know I've done bad in the past but that's behind me, 'onest.'

'I put it to you that you knew the area around Pinder Terrace was virtually deserted and you were not so much overcome by a full bladder that you had to urinate – less than 100 yards from the public house you had just left, incidentally – but rather that you sensed an opportunity and, being a serial thief, you couldn't resist, could you?'

'That's not true!' Thacker's voice rose.

'So, you relieved yourself – there is forensic evidence to that effect – and, as you lit a cigarette, you banged your body against the shed wall deliberately, to check for any reaction…'

'Rubbish!'

'… and then you didn't trip on the ramp at all, did you? You fell quite deliberately against the shed door, hoping that it would come open and you might find something worth stealing. That's what really happened, isn't it, Mr Thacker?'

Thacker shook his head and scowled. 'I shouldn't 'ave to listen to this crap. I'm the victim 'ere.'

'Mr Thacker,' the judge frowned, 'I appreciate that this is difficult for you but please answer the question.'

'I've told you what 'appened, Your Honour, and it's the truth.'

Matthews: 'Be honest, Mr Thacker: you turned and ran when you heard a voice from the shed not simply because you had been injured but because you knew you had been caught in the act and if the police found out, you would be going back to prison?'

'All I knew was I'd been cut by summat and I just wanted to get out of there, fast as I could.'

'Thank you, Mr Thacker, that will be all.'

The prosecutor resumed, 'Mr Thacker, so that the jury can be absolutely clear, do you feel that on the night in question you did anything wrong?'

'Apart from 'avin' a pee, no. I definitely di'n't deserve to be stabbed.'

Dessaur: 'Members of the jury, that concludes the case for the prosecution.'

*

COLIN Goodacre sellotaped shut a large envelope containing the week's penultimate batch of copy, layouts and photographs and tossed it to office junior Roy Dunne, whose job it was to put it on a bus to the printworks. It was Thursday morning and the *Bugle* would be on sale in less than 24 hours.

The editor sketched the front page on a sheet of A3 paper, leaving the top half for the splash. He wrote a working headline – 'Why I stabbed shed intruder' – and calculated the space it would fill in two lines of 90pt Franklin Gothic Condensed capitals, a font he reserved for major stories. Then he drew one box for Tommy's photograph and another for 400 words from Thursday's proceedings, which Simon had been told to phone through to the printers by 3pm that day.

Whether that space would be occupied by Tommy's evidence, due to be heard on Thursday morning, or Eddie Thacker's from the previous day remained to be seen. Either way, it would be worth front-page billing.

Managing director Walter Harding's ring-around the newsagents had found every one of them willing to take extra copies. It promised to be a bumper week for circulation.

THERE was no sign of Jean or Annie in the gallery when court resumed on Thursday morning and no sooner had the jury filed in than the reason became clear.

'Ladies and gentlemen,' said the judge, 'I regret to say that you have had a wasted journey. I am informed that the defendant is unwell and the trial cannot therefore continue today. Please enjoy your day off but remember that you must not discuss this case in the meantime. You may go now and I will see you back here at 10.30am tomorrow.'

Turning to the press bench, he added, 'Members of the press, I am happy for you to report that the trial has been adjourned for the day on my direction but nothing else, is that clear?'

'Bugger!' Simon muttered as the reporters filed out of court. 'Biggest case I've ever covered and we'll miss our deadline. Your lot'll have milked the old bloke's story before we get a sniff at it – that's all presuming he's well enough to continue.'

He had just enough money for ten cigs, his bus fare back to Brexham and two phone calls. First, the editor. 'Bloody typical,' sighed Colin. 'I'll have to rejig the front. Ah well, can't be helped. Get yourself back here, mate, and you can help us with a few bits for next week's paper.'

Simon pushed the other 10p into the slot at the sound of Jean's voice.

Tommy had seemed fine when he got up, she said, but over breakfast had complained of chest pains. 'He were sweating and seemed short of breath,' Jean gushed. 'I thought 'e were 'aving a 'eart attack, so I called t'doctor and 'e got an ambulance round. Was 'ere in about ten minutes.

'So, they took him to t'general 'ospital – I went with 'im, like – and they checked 'im out and said 'is 'eart seemed fine. Doctor asked if 'e'd been under any stress lately, so I told 'im t'situation and 'e said 'e were 99 percent sure it were a panic attack.

'Dad seemed much better after that. You know 'ow 'e makes out he's a tough nut but I reckon everything's just got to 'im. Doctor told 'im to take it easy and said 'e should be fine after a night's rest.'

'Phew, that's good news,' said Simon, feeling slightly guilty that he was more concerned about the story than Tommy's health. 'Send him my good wishes.'

Back at the office, reporter Gary Bostock had a message for him. It was from Welsh Rosie, who barmaided at the Unicorn when not giving hand relief at Mike's

Sauna. She had become a good contact since Simon's article on her grandparents' golden wedding anniversary.

'Reckons she's got a front-pager for you,' Gary said. 'Some old-timer was walking home from the pub when he coughed and his gnashers shot out and went down a drain. They're the best pair he's had, apparently, and he wants the council to suck them out for him. Rosie said to ring her and she'll give you his name and address.'

'Thanks,' Simon laughed. 'I love this job!'

*

JIM Richardson used the impromptu break from court to endure afternoon sex with Eunice. After Tracey, it was like swapping champagne for lemonade. If only his wife would show some initiative! But, as always on these rare occasions, he had to do it all – and he gave it his best, even going down on her until he detected a whimper of pleasure, then riding her until he was almost raw.

It was worth it in a way. Eunice made them a cup of tea afterwards and asked what had brought that on.

'I'll have trouble concentrating at the WI meeting tonight,' she giggled.

He cooked them sausage, fried egg and chips, with Arctic Roll for dessert, and they were sharing a bar of Old Jamaica while watching *Nationwide* on TV when he raised the prospect of selling Pinder Terrace and joining his old mate up in Whitby.

'I think we should, Jim,' she said. 'A fresh start might be just what we need. As long as we don't upset Mr Jepson. He's been there so long and never been any bother, bless him. I'd hate to think of him moving before he's ready.'

'Of course not, love,' he soothed. 'I'm happy for him to be there as long as he likes. But I'm afraid the matter might be taken out of our hands by the jury.'

He sighed as she touched his cheek. 'Oh well, Jim,' she said, 'you're just doing your job.'

*

FRIDAY morning found Tommy back in the dock. Annie squeezed Jean's hand and rolled her eyes as he replied 'yes, thank you, Your Honour' with a pronounced H when asked if he was feeling better.

The public gallery was packed once more and an extra figure had squeezed on to the press bench: a plummy type from *The Times*.

Tommy declined to swear the oath on the Bible but asked to affirm instead, and Simon flinched slightly, wondering if juries frowned on defendants who were not God-fearing, or admired them for sticking to their principles.

'Tell us about your house, Mr Jepson,' James Matthews began. 'Have you lived there long?'

'Thirty years,' said Tommy, his voice quivering slightly. He took a deep breath and continued firmly. 'Moved in with Rose – that's my late wife – and stayed ever since.'

'But you're now on your own?'

'Aye, sadly, since Rose passed, ooh, six year ago.'

'And you plan to continue living there, do you?

'Well, I did. I'm not so sure now, after all this. I knew I'd 'ave to move eventually cus they're building a road through it. But I thought I'd be there till t'bulldozers arrived and t'council found me a new place.'

'What happened to change your mind?'

'Well, about five months back, I got a brick through mi front window. A few weeks later, one through t'bathroom. Then this parcel came through t'letter box while I were out – human excrement, it was, as I soon discovered. Wrapped in newspaper, would you believe?'

There were murmurs from the jury.

'Please continue,' said the barrister.

'Nothing 'appened for a while after that. Then there were a dead pigeon hung on mi clothes line and I come home one day to find paint had been thrown on mi shed. That were bad enough but what really got to me were when the shed started shaking.'

'Please tell the jury what happened.'

'Well, I were in there one night, about nine o'clock it would've bin, and I 'eard footsteps going by and then suddenly, bang! They must've bin kickin' or thumping t'walls cus they started to shake and a pot o' varnish fell off a shelf.'

'Did you hear a voice from outside?'

'A youngish bloke's voice, aye. Couldn't make it all out but I 'eard him shout "get out o' there".'

'And how did you feel?'

'Bloody furious – sorry, Your Honour – and scared, if I'm 'onest.'

'Mr Jepson, have you any enemies, to your knowledge?'

'Not that I know of.'

'Any reason that you can think of why someone would want you out of your home?'

'I guess landlord'd be 'appy, as council'd have to buy it off 'em wi' me gone.'

Seated behind the lawyers, DI Richardson tensed.

'Your Honour!'

'Yes, Mr Dessaur?' said the judge.

'Your Honour, the landlord, whoever that might be, is not in the dock and it is highly inappropriate for any aspersions to be cast in that direction.'

'Objection upheld,' said the judge. 'The jury will kindly ignore that remark.'

Tommy looked affronted.

'Please tell us more about this outbuilding of yours,' Matthews continued. 'It seems to be rather important to you, considering that you were in there late at night.'

'It's mi second 'ome, you might say. I'm a bit of a carpenter. I make little things for mi granddaughter and 'er mates – jewellery boxes, puppets, that sort o' thing. Other bits I give to t'miners' welfare and they sell 'em for charity.'

Arise SaintbleedingThomas, Richardson thought.

Matthews: 'Do you sleep there, in the outbuilding?'

'Very rare, until recent. After the paint business and then the walls shakin', I started sleepin' there regular. It were just at the start o' that really 'ot spell and it were plenty warm enough. Besides, I've got water and electric and an old sofa in there, so I slept quite comfy on that.'

'What were your intentions in sleeping there?'

'To keep an eye on things, o' course. I didn't want mi work to be damaged. Plus, I've got some decent tools in there.'

'Tell us about the sword, Mr Jepson.'

'It were mi dad's. It's a dress sword, apparently, from some regiment or other. Story goes that 'e got drunk at a pub one night, took this sword off the wall while 'e were muckin' about and woke up next morning to find it by 'is bed.'

There was a ripple of laughter in the gallery.

'So, he phoned t'pub next morning to apologise and they told 'im 'e could keep it. Well, it were 'idden away for donkeys' years and I'd almost forgotten about it till I came across it in a drawer while I were doin' some clearin' out.'

'So how did it come to be in the shed on the evening of June the third?'

'I thought I'd clean it up and see if I could sell it. Thought I might get a few quid for it – put it up for auction at t'welfare, perhaps. So I'd been rubbing it down wi' wire wool and sandpaper cus it were pitted and rusty and…'

'Do we really need to know the history and condition of the sword, Your Honour?' the prosecutor interjected.

'Please get to the point, Mr Matthews,' the judge said, quietly pleased with his pun.

'Now,' the QC resumed. 'Tell us what happened on the evening of June the third.'

Tommy took a deep breath. 'Well, I'd been up there since five-ish and 'ad not long put mi light out and settled down to go to sleep. I were still in mi wheelchair cus I were feeling a bit weary. Sometimes I stay in it if I can't be bothered to get on to t'sofa.

'I were beginning to doze off when I 'eard a noise, a splashing sound, then a sort of a grunt.'

'Could you tell where this noise came from?'

'Only that it were nearby, cus I could 'ear it clearly. I weren't too bothered at that stage. Thought it might be someone 'avin' a slash on his way 'ome. You get a few using that alley as a short cut.'

'Go on.'

'Well, after what 'appened, I were nervous, so I switched this little torch on that I keep wi' me and I grabbed the sword – I'd left it on t'workbench next to me – and I pointed it at the 'ole where the letterbox should be…'

'Can I stop you just there, Mr Jepson? You have a letterbox in this outbuilding?'

Tommy laughed. 'Aye, well, the original door were damaged and this one were from a 'ouse that were being done up. But the letterbox flap were missing and I never got round to filling the 'ole up.'

'Tell us why you pointed the sword in the way you did.'

'I were worried someone might try to break in and do me some 'arm. I just wanted to protect meself. Next thing, the wall shook, like someone 'ad barged against it.'

'How did you feel at that moment?'

'Terrified. They could've 'ad a knife, a gun, or owt.'

'And then?'

'It all 'appened in a flash. There were an almighty thud on t'door and me arm were jabbed back, like summat 'ad 'it the sword. I shouted "clear off!" Then I 'eard a scream and footsteps running away and I waited a few minutes. Then I switched t'light on an' I could see blood on t'point o' t'sword.'

'Please continue, Mr Jepson.'

'I just sat there, frozen like, tryin' to work out what'd 'appened. I were still sat like that when Wendy – PC Marshall – and another bobby appeared.'

'Mr Jepson,' the barrister continued, 'I want to be clear about this because it's very important: why did you take hold of the sword that night?'

'To protect meself, that's all.'

'Had you ever intended to use it as a weapon?'

'No, sir.'

'Did you mean to hurt the man you had heard outside your shed?'

'No, never, and I feel sorry for t'lad, 'onest.'

'Thank you, Mr Jepson. Mr Dessaur might have some questions.'

Tommy pulled a large white handkerchief from his blazer and mopped his brow.

'Are you feeling all right?' asked the judge.

'Thank you, yes, Your Honour. But I could do with a drink of water.'

An usher obliged and the prosecutor rose to cross-examine.

'Mr Jepson,' he said warmly, 'I suspect that there is not a person in this court who does not sympathise with you over the vandalism you suffered in the weeks and months preceding this incident.

'But,' his tone changed, 'you were out for revenge, were you not?'

'No.'

'And you inflicted a serious wound with a deadly weapon.'

'Accidentally, aye, but that's all.'

'You are not seriously telling us, are you, given all that had gone before, that you innocently spent a night in the dark in your garden shed in a virtually deserted street, with a three-foot sword close to hand, with no intention of using it against someone you might perceive to be an intruder?'

'I'm telling you that because it's the truth.'

'Isn't the truth that you hadn't merely taken the sword to the shed to clean it up but to use it as a weapon to defend yourself?'

'That's not why I took it but I'm not going to lie' – his barrister winced, as ever on hearing such words from a client – 'I thought it might come in 'andy to scare 'em off if they came back.'

'You were going to teach the vandal, whoever it was, a lesson if he or she should come calling again. That's what you intended, isn't it? You told WPC Marshall as much immediately after you'd caused the injury to Mr Thacker's arm. "I'd just had enough." That's what you told her, isn't it?'

'Yes, but...'

'And who could blame you? Your house and your shed had been attacked – your workshop, where you engaged in your admirable endeavours to spread a little happiness. And then there were the incidents with the dead bird and the human excrement. You must have been furious, and indeed you have said so in this court. It would have tried the patience of a saint. And while you waited, in vain, for the police to catch the villain, your anger and frustration mounted, did they not?'

'Tell you t'truth, I 'oped it 'ad gone away.'

'But it gnawed away at you, didn't it, so much so that you thought if the police weren't going to do something, you would? And so you took the law into your own hands.'

'Not true.'

'You've told us that you pointed the sword at the hole where the letterbox should be. The truth is that that hole was perfect for your plan, wasn't it? You could wait behind the closed door, knowing that you could push the sword through the hole at any moment, and that's what you did. Isn't that the case?'

'I never intended to push it through the 'ole, as you put it. I were just restin' it there, just in case.'

'Mr Jepson, I'd like to take you back to the moment you first became aware that someone was outside the shed. You heard what you assumed to be someone urinating, yes?'

'Correct.'

'And you immediately reached for a deadly weapon! Why? Did it strike you, in that instant, that someone relieving themselves, say, on the way home from the pub might suddenly become an intruder?'

'I didn't know what might happen, after all t'trouble I'd 'ad.'

'And by the time Mr Thacker had tripped, muttered something and fallen against the door, you had pushed the point of the sword through the hole and into the man's arm. Was that not rather rash?'

'I told you, it all 'appened so sudden. I didn't 'ave time to think in case 'e broke t'door down. I couldn't see owt in t'dark. But I di'n't *push* it into 'is arm, 'e must've *fallen* on it, that's why mi arm were jabbed back.'

'But why not shout a warning to let the person know you were in there? Wouldn't that have been the sensible thing, if all you wanted to do was to scare him off?'

'It might've been, aye. But it would've advertised the fact I were in there.'

'The truth is that you didn't do either of those things because that would have taken away the element of surprise. And you didn't want that, did you, because it would have denied you the opportunity to do what you fully intended if the person you thought had caused you so much misery ever returned, and that was to teach him a lesson?'

Tommy shook his head vigorously. He could think of nothing more to say.

'Thank you, Mr Jepson, that's all for now.'

'Do you wish to re-examine, Mr Matthews?' said the judge.

'Very briefly, Your Honour. Mr Jepson, did you intend to hurt the man?'

'Never.'

'And did you think that by taking hold of the sword and pointing it towards the door you might cause him serious injury?'

'I swear on mi life, no.'

'Members of the jury, that is the case for the defence.'

*

TOMMY'S anxiety was clear during the lunch break. Jean told him to stop fidgeting. Tommy said he just wanted it over with, whatever the outcome

But, as the afternoon session began, it appeared that judge and barristers were keen to make an early start to the weekend.

Closing speeches by prosecution and defence were brief.

Prosecutor Gerald Dessaur was first to address the jury.

'I ask you,' he said, 'not to let your judgement be clouded by the fact that the defendant is an elderly and disabled gentleman but to consider what happened as a result of his actions.

'There is no disputing that he caused a very serious injury – one, as you have heard, that could have cost Mr Thacker his life had he not been given prompt first aid at the scene.

'Did the defendant intend to cause serious harm? If so, you must find him guilty of wounding with intent. If you are convinced, however, that he caused the injury recklessly – that is, without giving any thought to what might happen – he is guilty of the lesser charge on the indictment, that of assault causing grievous bodily harm.'

Defence counsel James Matthews submitted that it would be ludicrous to ignore Tommy's personal circumstances.

'It is easy for you and I,' he told the jury, 'relatively young and fit, to say that if we had been in Mr Jepson's shoes, we would have switched a light on or shouted as soon as we were aware of a noise outside, confident that this alone would have scared off whoever it was.

'But we are talking of an elderly gentleman who is confined to a wheelchair and who had every reason to think that not only his property but his life may be in danger.

'He was terrified. He acted in a moment of blind panic, and is that not an entirely understandable reaction?

'On both of the charges before you, a defendant is entitled to be acquitted if he acted in self-defence or defence of his property.'

As the lawyers sat back, their work done, Judge Widdowson said, 'Ladies and gentlemen of the jury, it is customary at this juncture for me to sum up the case before you and ask you to retire to consider your verdicts. However, I do not wish you to feel under any undue pressure to come to a decision. This is a very important case and you must be given a reasonable time to deliberate.

'Given the hour, I intend to adjourn for the day so that when you return on Monday morning and I remind you of the salient points of the case, they will be fresh in your minds when I send you out. I hope you have an enjoyable weekend.'

*

SATURDAY began with the promise of sunshine as the Richardsons set off for Whitby and a weekend stay as guests of Chief Superintendent Jim Pullman and his wife. But rain was falling in stair rods as they passed Pickering and drove across the North Yorkshire moors.

Tracey Beresford spent the morning more hindered than helped by Lucy as she baked fairy cakes and thought of her policeman lover. A feeling that it might be time to call it a day had been gnawing at her. Much as she loved being with him, she wanted, needed more than a few hours a week when he could fit her in.

A lunchtime session in the Unicorn had merely whet Flick's appetite and three beery pals eagerly followed him back to his caravan, with several quart bottles of IPA from the off-sales and a hanger-on in the form of Eddie Thacker, who had booked his ticket with a lump of hash hidden in his tobacco pouch.

Annie Shaw was engrossed in a Catherine Cookson novel at her new flat. Occasionally, she walked to the kitchen to stretch her legs and look out at the sparrows and starlings feasting at her bird table from Tommy.

Simon spent the afternoon watching TV with his grandfather. Fred Bains had come to stay for the weekend. To help out, he'd said. Lynne had laughed. Now she had another child to look after.

'I can manage,' she said when Simon half-heartedly offered to help with the shopping. 'It'll be nice for you two to spend some time together.'

Simon made them builders' tea and hand-cut Hovis with thick ham and English mustard and settled down on his mother's old settee beside the man who raised her.

For the next two hours, they barely spoke, content to be in each other's company and enjoy their lifelong love of sport as the day's football, tennis, boxing and rugby unfolded on *Grandstand*.

Simon rested his head on the shoulder of this big, strong man who had always seemed invincible. 'How are you coping, Grandad?'

'Not too bad, son,' Fred smiled.

But there was something missing about him since his little girl had gone, and Simon sensed that his childhood hero was only human after all.

16

JUDGE Widdowson prided himself on his scrupulously fair summings-up and today would be no exception. The national press was watching.

He led the jury through what few hard facts there were and the evidence of the various witnesses, pausing several times to stress that it was entirely a matter for the jury as to who they believed.

But, as always in high-profile cases, he had a nugget for the watching reporters.

'You may well have heard the phrase "an Englishman's home is his castle",' he said. 'Indeed, as recently as 1811, a citizen of this country was knighted for killing four burglars with a carving knife. One suspects that our current monarch might take a slightly different view.

'Ladies and gentlemen of the jury, you must approach this case with the utmost care and examine the prosecution and defence cases with great attention to detail, for to cause serious injury with a weapon is very wrong and the injured party may never regain full use of a limb.

'Equally, a man's home is sacrosanct and if he chooses to spend it for a period of time in a modest outbuilding, then that is his right.

'Now, please go and discuss the case among yourselves. Take all the time you need to reach verdicts on which you are all fully agreed and I will see you again when you are ready.'

*

EDDIE Thacker had to admit it: that Irish landlady was one smart cookie. He had never given the idea much thought, but Mary O'Sullivan had arranged for him to get some free advice from her solicitor.

'Oh yes,' the lawyer said, 'I think you might well qualify for a payment from what's called the Criminal Injuries Compensation Board – that's if this Mr Jepson of yours is found guilty.

'And it's not unheard of for compensation to be awarded in cases of acquittal. The board might consider that an injury caused by a sword, even if accidentally, is sufficient to justify an award – although you have admitted to committing a minor criminal offence, ie, urinating in a public place, which might weigh against you. And I'm afraid you'd be on a loser if you were to be charged with attempted burglary as a result of the incident.'

That prospect had worried Eddie initially but, as he awaited the jury's verdicts, seated as far as possible from Tommy's table in the foyer of Shire Hall, he recalled the words of the police officer who had interviewed him shortly before the trial: the evidence against him, he'd said, was so flimsy that it would probably be laughed out of court.

For a copper, Eddie thought, Detective Inspector Richardson seemed a decent bloke.

*

TOMMY made small talk with Jean, Annie and Simon while his future hung in the balance.

It was shortly before 11.30am and the court rarely sat beyond 4.30pm, so even if the jury came back today, he might be on tenterhooks for five hours. He'd read of juries taking days to come back because they couldn't agree. Then what? There might be a retrial and he'd have to go through it all over again.

Annie was chatting excitedly about her new flat, though Simon had been inside already and Jean felt she knew the place from his report in the paper, the one headlined 'Plucky pensioner wins David and Goliath battle'.

Tommy felt the voices drifting further away. Small beads of perspiration broke out on his brow – not the sweat of a stuffy old court building on a hot day, but the cold sweat of anxiety.

There were twinges of pain in his chest and a tingling in his fingers. He took deep, steady breaths and chastised himself for the looming signs of what he now recognised as a panic attack.

Panic? Puh! After all he'd gone through? After all the years of danger he'd endured underground; after the amputations and the loss of his dear Rose. 'Pull yourself together, man!' he told himself.

Barely three hours had passed when James Matthews hurried to their table. 'The jury's coming back,' he said.

'Is that good or bad?' Annie whispered as they filed into court.

'Could be either,' said Simon. 'It probably just means they're in no doubt.'

*

TOMMY leaned forward as the clerk asked the jury foreman to stand.

'On the first count on the indictment,' she began, 'of causing grievous bodily harm with intent, have you reached a verdict on which you are all agreed?'

'We have, Your Honour.'

Tommy gripped the arms of his wheelchair.

'Do you find the defendant, Thomas Elijah Jepson, guilty or not guilty?'

'Not guilty.'

'And on the second count, of causing grievous bodily harm, do you find him guilty or not guilty?'

'Not guilty.'

Cheers and applause broke out in the gallery. Judge Widdowson raised an arm to quell them. 'Mr Jepson,' he said. 'You are free to go, without a stain on your character. However, you may wish to hear what I have to say.

'I have been deeply concerned to discover, during the course of this trial, that a vulnerable, elderly man was left to live in isolation in a clearance area for a significant period of time.

'It is abundantly clear that the suffering endured by both Mr Jepson and Mr Thacker would have been avoided if action had been taken to prevent the conditions that existed in Pinder Terrace, and I shall be making my views known to the relevant authorities.'

*

THAT evening…

Eddie Thacker was interviewed at Solly's Transport Café and Lodging House by the man from the *Mirror*. He was to receive £100 for his story. After all, the reporter said, Eddie had not been charged with an offence, which made him an innocent man. He had been stabbed with a sword and nearly lost his life. And the man who did it had got off scot-free. 'Too bloody right,' said Eddie.

DI Richardson's day went from bad to worse. He called Clive Pullman to say he should be able to make the move to Whitby before long. But Pullman told him his DI had decided to put off his retirement for a year. 'I'm sorry, Jim,' he said. 'Just hang on a bit longer, pal. The job's yours as soon as he gives in his ticket.'

Tommy declined the offer of a celebration party at the miners' welfare. It was a nice thought, he said, but probably tomorrow. All he wanted was a quiet night in. He felt more tired than at any time in his life.

Annie caught a bus to Jean's to deliver a steak and kidney pudding, which Tommy devoured, along with a mountain of Jean's mashed potatoes and soggy cabbage, just the way he liked it.

Then he retired to his makeshift bedroom with his Ella Fitzgerald tapes, a bottle of Mackeson and his hip flask of single malt.

*

A LIE-IN was one thing, Jean thought the next morning, but 11 o'clock was taking the mickey. She went to rouse Tommy and found him curled up in the foetal position, eyes closed, stone dead.

Keith Boam's mobile grocery shop, parked in the street nearby, was busy with customers when the ambulance arrived. From there the news spread rapidly through the close-knit community and was soon the talk of Brexham Police Station.

DI Richardson phoned his wife with the news.

'I feel a bit guilty, love,' he said.

'Aww, Jim,' she soothed, 'you couldn't do anything about it.'

By the time Annie and WPC Marshall had been and gone amid tea and tears, Jean had slammed the phone down on three tabloid newspapers, astonished at how quickly the news had reached them.

It would be two days before she felt able to talk without breaking down.

As Colin Goodacre sweated over what his front page would say, Jean finally phoned Simon. There would have to be a postmortem, she said, but initial tests suggested Tommy had suffered a massive stroke.

'I reckon that panic attack was probably an early warning sign,' she said, 'but don't put that in t'paper.'

'Of course not, love. But would you like to say anything about what Tommy had to go through?'

'What can I say? It's shocking, i'n't it? He should never've been charged in t'first place. The poor bloke's name's been dragged through t'mud and he's had to wait months to be cleared. And after all that, he's not even lived a day to enjoy it. I reckon all the pressure of the arrest and the trial just finished him off.'

Then she said the three words that gave the editor the headline he had hoped for: 'CALL THAT JUSTICE?'

CHAPTER TWO

1

IN the fusty living room of his one-bedroom flat with its drawn curtains and its carpet of newspaper cuttings and council reports, Frank Noon sat down with a cup of tea and reached for the inevitable.

The letter from Transport House, Labour Party HQ, came as no surprise. Even so, seeing it in black and white filled him with sadness.

He was expelled from the party forthwith, it said. The National Executive Committee had rejected his final appeal. His offence: continued public opposition to party policy regarding the Brexham Town Traffic Corridor Scheme.

Frank had hoped – had fully expected – that when Labour seized back control of the borough council six months after Tommy Jepson's death, the project he had fought so passionately would be buried once and for all.

He had reckoned without the new clique of college types among Labour councillors, swept in at the polls and now outnumbering old socialists like himself who earned a living by getting their hands dirty.

The party's top brass had been sorely embarrassed by the Jepson affair. Judge Widdowson's comments had sparked national publicity and the old man's death had thrust the town and its rulers on to the front pages. 'KILLED BY RED TAPE' screamed one. Questions were asked in parliament.

With Labour in charge of both local authorities, no one else could now be blamed for the road debacle, and the full weight of the party machine descended on them, making the project party policy.

It was too late to turn back, they said.

Two wrongs never made a right, said Frank.

You've had your say, they said. Now shut up.

He walked over to his dusty sideboard, picked up a framed photograph of his late father, smiling beside Ramsay MacDonald during the coal strike of 1912, and brought it close to his face.

'Thirty-eight years I've been a party man, Dad. Ever since you signed me up on my 16th birthday, remember? Always honoured majority decisions, I have, even when I disagreed with 'em. Just like others did when the boot was on the other foot. As you used to say, without party discipline, there'd be anarchy.'

But on this one issue Frank could not give in. How could he turn his back on the electors to whom he had sworn undying opposition to the road? It would be an insult to Tommy's memory, an insult to all those still alive and suffering upheaval in the name of the road, to pretend that it was not a huge, expensive mistake after all.

He had taken his opposition to the top, sending a dossier to the prime minister, Jim Callaghan, complete with photographs showing the route cleared of houses and small business premises. Why not build new homes there, he asked. Put people back into the town. Create a thriving community in reach of the shops, the bingo hall, the cinema.

A standard letter of acknowledgement was all it got him.

All those Labourites who had shared his stance in opposition – people like Ken Farnsworth, a man he had regarded as a friend and who now found himself leader of the borough council – had not only gone back on their word but had punished Frank for sticking to his. Farnsworth had even seconded the expulsion motion at a constituency meeting.

They were the guilty ones. They had betrayed the public to save their political skins.

Frank knew only too well that his choice left him in the political wilderness, unable to call on party colleagues for support on issues close to his heart. They would see him as a pariah and oppose him for the hell of it. He had seen it happen often enough to others. All he could hope was that the Tories, knowing what a thorn in the administration's side he could be, might give him a committee seat here and there.

But what could a lone voice hope to achieve? Getting overcrowded families rehoused was tough enough when he had the party behind him. What chance now?

How easy would it be now for housing director Howard Wragg and his surly sidekick, Gordon Grebby, to brush off complaints about tenants' damp walls, rotting window frames and faulty heating?

Well, Frank thought, I might not have power but I can still be a bloody nuisance.

He pulled on his beige corduroy blazer, stuffed a brown envelope into one pocket and a bag of breadcrumbs into the other, then pressed 'play' on his trusty cassette recorder, slid the machine into his trademark rucksack, gently pressed the earphones into position and stepped outside.

*

PASSERS-BY might have thought 'him off the council' was replaying Tony Benn's latest speech or the highlights of a Sewers and Grass Verges Sub-committee meeting. It tickled Frank to think what they would say if they knew his eardrums were being assailed by crashing cymbals and thudding bass lines.

There was the hint of a smile and a skank as he mouthed to a Desmond Dekker number, 'Wake up in the morning, slaving for bread, sir, so that every mouth can be fed...'

He thought of all the grumbling and insults he suffered from voters who believed all councillors were the same: only in it for what they could get. True, there were some bad apples but he still clung to the belief that most set out with good intentions, determined to help their fellow citizens, to make their little corner of the world a better place. Some, though, like Farnsworth, were seduced by power and became the problem, not the solution; they stopped sticking up for the people against the system and became the system.

'A corrupted man's heart is a ghetto,' the earphones boomed, 'a righteous man's heart is a paradise.'

Transcendental meditation, brown rice, Christianity, homoeopathy, spiritualism, hypnotherapy, the I Ching, Chairman Mao's Little Red Book. Frank had tried them all in his quest for Oneness, Contentment and the Wider Picture since his wife left him for someone who cared more for her than town hall politics: another woman.

Now he found comfort in reggae. A friend of Simon's had introduced him to it after a lunchtime drinking session that spilled over to a flat where speakers that took up half a wall boomed out Jamaican sounds and slugs of white rum oiled conversations that put the world to rights and quickly forgot where they were heading.

There was hardly a black face in Brexham, let alone a ready supply of reggae records, but Frank would take a train to Birmingham, then a bus to Handsworth, where he would seek out red, gold and green album sleeves in hazy shops populated by large Rastafarians who eyed him with a mixture of suspicion and amusement.

Back home, he transferred the vinyl to tape and began impersonating the patois of reggae toasters. Amid the humour were snippets of working-class philosophy he could relate to. One day, he had promised himself, he would perform a Rastafarian monologue at a Labour Party social. No chance of that now.

*

THE moment Frank set foot on the Morbury Canal towpath, just a few hundred yards from his front door, the world seemed a better place.

No one would call it an area of outstanding natural beauty but it was Brexham's, and townsfolk young and old had been better able to enjoy its charms since volunteers had cleared a three-mile stretch of abandoned bicycles, oil drums and sofas and made the waterway navigable once more.

Flanked by sycamores and weeping willows, the ancient trading route linked to a network of canals to the south and east and welcomed narrowboats with names like Little John and Pride of Yorkshire.

Cleaner water meant more fish and the canal had become a magnet for maggot fishermen and serious anglers alike; a summertime swimming pool for gypsy kids and a year-round escape for those content to stroll along its banks and commune with its flourishing wildlife.

The canalside was also a gateway to acres of fields and woodland, criss-crossed by rough footpaths and bridleways and dotted with stiles and streams, where one could lose oneself for hours, away from car horns, factory fumes and the grind of daily life.

But even this little corner of paradise could not push politics out of mind today, for Frank's expulsion had given him a new opponent: Tommy Jepson's daughter, Jean Palethorpe.

He had watched with admiration as Jean put herself forward for public service, inspired by the sense of injustice that had grown throughout her father's harassment and trial.

Labour were glad to have her as a candidate and Frank signed her nomination forms. Jean won her seat comfortably and he looked forward to having a new ally.

Instead, the road opened a chasm between them and, though they might still exchange pleasantries, the old stager knew how things worked; knew that novice councillors relied on senior figures for support and guidance as they settled in; knew that if it came to the crunch, Jean would line up with his former comrades and vote against him.

He pulled the bag of breadcrumbs from his pocket and a feathered flotilla headed his way. They recognised him instantly, of that he had no doubt, and among this quacking, squawking fraternity, Frank had discerned a range of personalities.

There were shy ducks and show-offs. There were drakes so daft that in chasing off others, they missed out on the breadcrumbs. There were bossy old biddies, and little moorhens that braved coots and geese to skedaddle across the water at the first hint of food and feast under the noses of huge swans too posh or short-sighted to appreciate the rambler's offerings.

And ever-present was a male duck missing a large chunk of its bill. This battered specimen would boldly climb the bank for food, briefly leaving its constant companions, a female and another male. Frank had dubbed him Split Bill and, in idle moments, found himself pondering on Bill's sexual proclivities, noting that it was always approaching females that he would chase away, as if he were a grandparent trying to save his son-in-law from temptation – or perhaps a sneaky love rival awaiting the chance to whisk the betrothed away one night while dad sang the babies to sleep with *Five Little Ducks Went Swimming One Day*.

In the fading light of a Friday evening, such musings carried him from rural tranquillity to the stir of a town centre pulling on its glad rags for the weekend.

Relieved to find the *Bugle* office closed and deserted, he wondered what would become of the fuse he was about to light as he pulled the brown envelope from his pocket, scrawled 'council corruption, FAO Simon Fox' on the front and pushed it through the letterbox.

Then he strode up the high street with a message from Bob Marley in his earphones:

So, if you are the big tree
We are the small axe
Ready to cut you down
To cut you down.

2

SATURDAY afternoon playtime was over and Lynne Fox planted a noisy kiss on the forehead of her two-year-old niece. 'Bye, gorgeous,' she beamed. 'Love you.'

'Lub you,' Angelica said with a gummy smile and returned to her dolls.

'You must be worn out, Lynne,' her sister laughed, helping her on with her coat. Two hours of singing, dancing and storytelling was harder than a day at work but Lynne wouldn't miss it for the world.

'Dunno how you keep up with her, Sylv,' she frowned. 'She's such a bundle of energy.'

'Don't worry,' Sylvia snorted, 'she doesn't get *that* much attention when you're not here. I'll be sticking her in front of the telly for an hour when you've gone. *Rainbow* works wonders! Anyway, when are you and Simon going to have one?'

'A baby? You must be joking! I hardly get time to breathe as it is. I'm off to see Mam now. Wants me to go help her pick a new blouse at the Co-op.'

It was true, she hardly had a minute to herself. She was either out at work or racing to keep home and family in order: washing, ironing, dusting, Hoovering, cooking, then making sure Dawn and Paul did their homework before they disappeared for the evening, leaving her to worry what they were up to while Simon was covering a parish council meeting or some other assignment for his precious newspaper.

She hugged her sister goodbye and enjoyed a secret cigarette on her walk to the Co-op. By the time she had seen her mum safely home from shopping, all she wanted to do was curl up on the settee and watch a little mindless TV with a can of Coke and a bar of chocolate. Instead, she would be getting dolled up to play the dutiful wife.

*

BREXHAM Borough Council's civic dinner and dance, at the Mecca Ballroom, was an opportunity to bury the harsh words and machinations of politics and enjoy a night out with fellow human beings.

There were old acquaintances to renew, jokes to share, contacts to make, secret flames to fan, allies to engage in mutual back-slapping, titbits to be whispered, the seeds of business deals to be sewn, enemies to greet with handshakes and smiles, and wine aplenty to wash down a five-course feast, courtesy of the ratepayer.

Even Madam Mayor Enoch, queen of the lemon-suckers, bared her teeth in vague imitation of a smile as she greeted Simon and Lynne with a cold fish of a handshake.

In the infancy of his hobnobbing career, Simon had viewed this annual shindig as a disgusting spectacle of greed but, with practice, had come to enjoy it, in a strange sort of way. The horrors of dressing like a penguin had waned with time as he learned, with alcoholic assistance, to unleash his charm on strangers intrigued by the combination of tuxedo and hippy hair.

The guest list had changed since last year, since Labour had wrested back control of the council. It was now their turn to reward and impress, though there was no sign of man of principle Frank Noon. There never was, and especially not now.

The politics might have changed but they all looked the same in their finery, Simon thought, as a Beatles song swam into his head:

Everywhere there's lots of piggies
Living piggy lives
You can see them out for dinner
With their piggy wives
Clutching forks and knives to eat the bacon!

And he was one of them.

In this arena, on this night, he was as good, or bad, as any of the town's elite, afforded courtesy by fellow diners, even those who privately loathed him or the press in general or both.

Still, it disturbed him to think that, for all his fancy talk and socialist ideals, he was no better than the rest of the 200 guests: a privileged freeloader.

In moments of generosity, he might have argued that they were all, in some small way, contributing to public life and the semblance of order that kept the parks tidy and the dustbins emptied. But there were never any gardeners or dustmen among the top cops and captains of industry, Rotarians and Round Tablers, shopkeepers, clergymen, publicans, party grandees and a chain gang of visiting mayors and mayoresses who slurped themselves half-cut in readiness for the twist and the conga that would surely arrive as midnight loomed and inhibitions slipped away.

The Foxes spent the meal in pleasant conversation with the Derringers. For all their wealth and breeding, the county's High Sheriff and his wife were remarkably down to earth.

Lynne cast Simon a discreet frown as he downed another second glass of wine. His eyebrows shrugged back. She was worried about his drinking. On nights out with their stoner friends, a couple of pints at the pub had progressed to five or six, followed by smoking sessions at one house or the other, where a few joints had turned into a production line.

They would swig rum and tequila until the combination of booze and dope left them spluttering and senseless with laughter, and from this state Simon would sometimes wake, oblivious, and pee anywhere other than in the toilet. Lynne had laughed about the stained wardrobe door and the dripping telephone receiver but was not amused when he mistook the fridge for the toilet one night, forcing her to bin a joint of beef and serve sausages instead when her parents arrived for Sunday lunch.

The toast and speeches over, an ant-like army of housewife waitresses earning pin money swooped to clear and re-lay tables in readiness for the serious business of drinking.

As ballroom favourites gave way to disco classics and the lights dimmed, Lynne pulled Cynthia Derringer on to the dancefloor and was soon bopping her heart out while Simon toured the room, buying and accepting drinks, pulling up a chair here and there and chatting to familiar faces in an unfamiliar setting.

He spotted Tory veteran Rose Sutton sitting alone and sidled up to her, pressing his thigh cheekily against hers. A reporter had his duty to do.

Rose was a nice old stick and he felt sorry for her. In the eloquent assessment of Frank Noon, her husband was the sort who would shag a rag doll.

'You ought to expose the bastard,' Frank had nagged. 'I could point you to two of his bits on the side straight away.'

As if widespread knowledge of her husband's philandering were not burden enough, Rose had lost most of her hair by the time she was 60, a secret rudely exposed at a council meeting when Frank, gesticulating to make a point, innocently caught his shirt cuff on her wig.

Simon bought her a G&T and was rewarded with a tip-off: Gordon Grebby, the assistant director of housing, was rumoured to be retiring early.

'It's only what I've heard,' Rose whispered. 'Don't say it came from me.'

'Of course not,' he winked. 'You know me, I'm the soul of discretion.'

Old Sourpuss going, eh? Hardly big news but it might make a paragraph or two.

3

GORDON Grebby closed the file marked 'Housing Department repairs account, second quarter', replaced the top on his gold-plated Parker pen, inscribed with 'For 25 years' loyal service', and looked out of his office window at the brick wall of the Borough Surveyor's Department.

He might be about to lose a large part of his life.

He answered the phone begrudgingly and bristled at the voice of a young man. It was 'that beatnik from the *Bugle*'.

Grebby disliked the press with a passion and viewed Simon Fox with a contempt he found difficult to disguise and harder still to reconcile with his Christian beliefs.

It was, he felt, indicative of falling standards wherever one looked that such an individual, with his long hair and his open collar, was afforded a place on the press bench at council meetings and a passport to dine and gossip with the town's rich and powerful at soirees from which the likes of Grebby were excluded.

He kept his calm as he responded to Simon's enquiry. No, he would not care to confirm or deny the so-called rumour that he was to retire early. 'As I'm sure you are well aware, Mr Fox, information about staffing matters is confidential, and any report about myself will be viewed very seriously. Do I make myself clear?' He did not wait for a reply.

Grebby took a few deep breaths. He was being squeezed. They wanted him out.

He was angry not so much at the phone call but at his foolishness in thinking he might one day be allowed to go with dignity. He had entered local government in an age when everyone batted for the same side, when confidentiality meant just that. There were so many spivs on the council these days! Even among the paid staff there was an element of politically active officers – the CND brigade, he called them – who viewed quiet, long-serving officers like himself with disdain and thought it acceptable to leak information when it suited them.

Well, he might soon be rid of the lot of them. No more smelly families invading his office to moan about broken window catches. No more kowtowing to jumped-up councillors, pleading for special treatment for their friends. No more taking orders from the likes of Howard Wragg, the archetypal modern director: wet behind the ears but full of management qualifications. No more being manipulated by an unholy alliance that stretched beyond the town hall into miners' welfare clubs and Masonic lodges and God knows where else and conspired to fudge democratic decisions and bend council policies.

He had seen what was coming. More and more work was being privatised. Before long, there would be no council houses left for him to manage.

That business of the heating contract had dispelled the last grains of doubt. He had put two and two together as soon as he had seen the report to committee. He had sent Wragg a memo, advising him to declare an interest and take no part in discussions about Sewter Heating. The director had not bothered to reply.

It was no secret that councillors were looking to cut the wage bill. A staff review had identified several senior posts that might go. Grebby had been approached. He had registered his interest, if the terms were right. That was as far as it had gone, and that was no business of the press.

He left the office on the stroke of five and walked pensively to St Andrew's Church for bell-ringing practice.

Retirement certainly had its attractions. He was 53 and not in the best of health. It would be nice to see more of his dear Marge and devote more time to serving the Lord, who had kept his sinful secret safe.

*

EVERY part of Mary Clitheroe's face looked as though it had had its teeth removed, though something resembling teeth lived on her bottom gum, bearing testimony to the day's meals.

'How's mi favourite newspaper man?' she squawked, flopping into a chair at Simon's table in the Station Hotel, where he had called for 'a quick one' on the way home.

He swiftly put away the sheet of beige paper he had been studying. Frank Noon had refused even to confirm that it had come from him, though his handwriting was suspiciously familiar, and Simon's other council contacts had been similarly tight-lipped.

It was difficult to get excited about the minutes of a meeting of the housing improvement sub-committee, which routinely met in private on the grounds that sensitive information about individuals and businesses might be discussed.

In a few short paragraphs, the document referred to complaints of damp homes on Darley Estate and recorded a decision to award Sewter Heating Ltd a £57,000 contract to fit electric storage heaters in selected properties, on the advice of the director of housing.

'There must be something fishy about it or I wouldn't have been tipped off – with "corruption" on the envelope,' Simon had told his editor. But Colin Goodacre had taken one look at the report and said, 'So where's the scandal? It says bugger all as it stands, buddy. Hardly worth a line, unless you can prove otherwise.'

'Don't mind if we join you, do you, mi darlin'?' Mary Clitheroe said, throwing back a head of greasy, tousled hair with a manic laugh and giving him a wink as if they were sharing some big secret.

Jesus, Simon thought. Why do I always attract the nutters?

Wherever Mary went, her sister Eileen went, too. Eileen with her warts and monobrow.

During drunken evenings, with their table full of empty pint pots and shot glasses, Simon and his pals would giggle as they debated what might persuade them to shag either of that grimy pair. A new Porsche was the nearest they came to agreement.

He happened to glance at the bar and caught Graham the Joiner grinning in his direction with a 'you're in there, son!' thumbs-up.

Graham was a creep. The sort who'd be all over you one minute and ignore you the next. The sort who always had his hands on other people's wives. The sort who sank five pints every night and drove home.

The sort who came up with a good story now and again.

Simon recalled his tip-off about a builder who had battered his mate to death and buried him in the garden of a house they were renovating.

He was being beckoned out of dreamland. Someone was gripping his arm. It was Eileen. Oh please, God, he thought, don't make me shag her. I was only joking about the Porsche.

'Ere duck,' she was saying? 'Ave y'eard owt about our 'eating? Only it's been rubbish since they put them storage things in last month.'

Defective heaters? A council contract? Grebby retiring? Was this, he wondered, mere coincidence?

'Y'ought to put summat in t'paper, mester,' Mary roared. 'Go on, tell 'im, Eileen.'

'OK,' he smiled, pulling out his notebook, 'come on, Eileen.'

*

THE Clitheroe sisters' complaints about their new storage heaters, which either failed to warm a room or cost a fortune to run, made a short piece on page 13 of the week's *Bugle*.

It was, after all, ten-a-penny stuff to a borough authority but Simon had been surprised when his call for a comment was put through to Howard Wragg himself, rather than the press office.

He could not have imagined the kerfuffle that followed.

Wragg had dictated a short statement, promising to investigate the problem of Eileen's pipes, then phoned Ken Farnsworth and drove the three miles to their golf club.

Before going inside, he studied himself in the mirror of his black Mercedes, lit up his tanned face with the gleaming smile of one who had always taken care of his teeth and combed a few stragglers into place on a fine head of blond hair that belied his 48 years.

Farnsworth, a thin, weasel of man man whose teenage acne had defied decades of creams and lotions, was waiting at a secluded table. 'Howard!' he boomed. 'Nice to see you out of the office.'

Wragg found the fact that Farnsworth was one of Brexham's most powerful men hard to stomach. He remembered when one needed real status to be a Mason. Nowadays they let anyone in. Farnsworth was not only chairman of the policy committee and consequently leader of the council, but worshipful grand master of the town's last remaining lodge. And a greengrocer to boot.

'Now,' the weasel's voice dropped, 'what's all this about? And why the secrecy, Howard? We've got a place for that, you know!'

Wragg cast a discreet eye around him and spoke softly, 'It's Grebby, Ken. We've got to get rid of him. I've heard he's spoken to that troublemaker from the paper. He could make waves.'

'Really? Old Sourpuss?' Farnsworth chuckled. 'We're looking at all that, Howard. But you know better than me how these things work. The staff review panel will report before Christmas. We can hardly jump the gun.'

'Well, you'd better start. Next year could be too bloody late.'

Farnsworth noted with quiet satisfaction that beads of perspiration had formed on the director's forehead. He was usually too damned smug by half.

'For God's sake,' Wragg said, 'give him what he wants and let him go. It could save us all a lot of unpleasantness.'

'Us?' Farnsworth raised his eyebrows. 'Now hang on, old friend. You landed yourself in this Sewter business, not us.'

'Yes, but you knew about it. If I'm at fault, you're guilty of a cover-up.'

'But it's the money, my friend. We can't magic it out of thin air.'

'Of course we can!' the director hissed. 'How do you think we get your party's pet schemes through after you've forgotten to budget for them? A little juggling of resources can work wonders.'

Wragg had been doing the sums since Grebby's memo had landed on his desk. The director could have kicked himself for his stupidity. He should have seen danger coming and declared an interest; should have known Grebby would make the connection. Checking out firms that tendered for contracts was his job, after all. If only he wasn't so bloody righteous!

It was not as if Wragg had profited financially. Sewter's tender was perfectly acceptable: the lowest of six received. But Wragg knew how it looked. So did Grebby and he was holding out for more in his retirement pot.

'You've got to understand, Ken,' he said calmly, 'if this goes wrong, it won't just be me who has something to worry about. You of all people know what the media's like. They'll think the whole authority's bent and try digging up all sorts of connections that people would rather keep to themselves.'

It was now the council leader's turn to squirm. He knew that Wragg knew of his ownership of two condemned houses along the road route. There was nothing sinister in that but it would do Farnsworth's socialist credentials no good at all if it came out.

'Do what you have to,' he sighed, 'but keep the settlement hush-hush. Any hint of preferential terms and the unions will do their nut.'

*

ARMED with two egg custard tarts from the Co-op, Frank Noon headed to Annie Shaw's for what had become a Friday morning fixture: an hour's chat over a cup of tea while she regaled him with neighbourhood gossip.

A copy of the *Bugle* was tucked under one arm. Each Friday, he would scour the newspaper from back to front, then pass it on, knowing that Annie still liked to count the pennies, even with a decent sum in the bank from the sale of her house in Pinder Terrace.

There was still nothing in it about the heating contract, nothing substantial at least. The Clitheroe sisters' story was a mere diversion. Frank knew that 'daft pair' well and chuckled at the thought of Simon trying to get some sense out of them.

If only he could give the reporter a comment, something for him to work on. But he was walking a tightrope. Dumped by Labour, his only hope of staying within sniffing distance of what really went on at the town hall was to cosy up to the Tories, and they, too, would wash their hands of him if they found he had broken council rules by leaking confidential information.

Painful as it might be, he could not afford to upset the party he had fought against all his adult life. Not yet. Once he had his feet under the table, perhaps.

*

IF Howard Wragg had been asked to define manna from heaven, Hilton's bra factory would never have entered his thoughts.

He had not heard of Linda Barclay and, as he twiddled his pen and watched the clock, two hours from the end of a dull day, the one name on his mind was that of Gordon Grebby. Weeks of discussion had brought them close to a settlement but the deputy director was still pushing for more.

A trim figure with a blonde bob, Linda lit a Woodbine the moment she passed Security on her way out of Hilton's, relieved to see the back of another four-day week of piecework.

She caught a bus into town and watched the passing world through rivulets of rain, her stomach fizzing with indignation at what she was about to do. But do it she would: she owed it to Hughie.

He had been such a fine catch: honest, hardworking, strong, yet gentle underneath the machismo, and she loved him all the more for his forgiveness.

They had been desperate for a child and, after three fruitless years, the headboard that once rattled with abandon increasingly fell silent as Hughie, racked by his failure to prove himself a man, withdrew into his shell, drinking heavily, exploding at the merest excuse into foot-stomping rages, and finding himself utterly incapable of getting an erection.

In the depths of misery, Linda had opened the door to a council official conducting a survey of housing conditions. He was ten years or so her senior, not much to look at, she thought, but smartly dressed and with a kind face.

When he called a second time to check some details, she was several gins to the good and still in her nightie at midday.

He was a good listener and they talked about schools and jobs and places they'd known. He made her laugh with stories of his young son. Then the laughter turned to tears as she opened her heart about her barren marriage.

She would never understand what possessed her next but she almost tore off his trousers and let him take her there and then, in front of the gas fire. It was not even good sex and, after the next time, he told her it had to end: he loved his family too much, and knew, as a Christian, that the affair was wrong.

The little shit! She told him to get out and made some remark about the size of his manhood. He stuttered apologies as he shuffled backwards out of the door, thanking her for 'you know', and she sobbed the afternoon away, more through guilt than rejection.

That night, she cuddled up to Hughie for the first time in weeks and whispered, 'I love you.'

One missed period was not the end of the world. The second confirmed what she already knew, and she confessed all to Hughie. His first thought was to strangle her. On reflection, he would chop her up and feed her to the dog.

After weeks of rows and tears, an idea budded and blossomed in his head as he tossed sleeplessly in the spare room: a thought that at last quelled the inner turmoil. Over cornflakes the next day, he cracked the icy silence that had descended on breakfast as regularly as the morning dew.

'Let's keep the baby,' he said.

It was, after all, what they had always wanted, the one thing missing from their lives. So, she had been a fool, but so had he. Their love was strong enough to carry them through, he said, and Linda wept in agreement. Save for a teaspoon of semen, every ingredient of their child would be theirs and the world would be none the wiser.

For 13 years, they rewrote the book of joy as Kelly grew from tot to teenager. They put her academic brilliance down to luck and laughed when people said she had her mother's looks. She was the perfect daughter, repaying their love over and again.

Linda vowed not to mention or set eyes on Gordon Grebby ever again, though she could not help but notice his name in the Bugle occasionally as he rose from humble housing inspector.

How their smart and sensible girl fell under the spell of that dirty, uncouth lot the Beresfords would perplex her parents to the grave. Kelly had always been so clean and particular. Flick's little sister Sharon seemed the unlikeliest of friends but the girls became inseparable.

It would be several months before Kelly's parents discovered that the pair of them had been skipping homework sessions in Sharon's bedroom and sneaking out to join a gang of roughnecks who gathered with motorbikes and transistor radios on street corners until, driven out by the police, they sought refuge in a disused clay pit, where Kelly swigged cider and sniffed glue and fell pregnant by one of a succession of greasy youths adept at exploiting the pangs of blooming sexuality.

Hughie considered suicide. He blamed himself for wrapping her in cotton wool. When the pain had given way to fury, he threatened to kick her out.

Now, it was Linda's turn to be strong, to save the family she had put at risk. The Beresfords were not going to ruin all she had worked for. Kelly, she vowed, would have an abortion, like it or not. There would be no more contact with Sharon and she would buckle down at school, do her O-levels and make something of her life.

First, they had to get her off the estate, away from temptation and into a new school. Kelly protested with all the passion and logic she could muster. She was roundly ignored. Hughie, too, was uneasy at the prospect of a move. He had spent his whole life in the same street and liked to joke that he would need a passport to leave. It was the right thing to do, he said, but it could take months or even years to get another council house.

You just watch, Linda thought, as the bus pulled to a halt outside the town hall.

'I've come to see the director of housing,' she announced.

'Do you have an appointment?' the receptionist sniffed.

'No, but I think he'll see me,' Linda said cockily. 'Just tell him it's about a delicate matter concerning one of his staff and if he won't see me, I'll go to the press.'

Fifteen minutes later, Howard Wragg was looking forward to removing the thorn of Gordon Grebby from his side with considerably more ease than he had expected. Pandering to the likes of 'that woman' was not something he was used to but he figured he had done himself no harm by sparing the council embarrassing publicity.

Linda, meanwhile, was on her way home, assured of a new council house within the month.

4

THERE was something unusual about Marge Grebby as she took her place in her usual pew for the Sunday morning service at St Andrew's Church: husband Gordon was not at her side.

Geraldine Merryweather was running late and had to sit one row back. She tapped her friend on the shoulder and swapped smiles before mouthing 'where is he?' as the Rev Peter asked the congregation to stand for Love Divine, All Love Excelling.

'Tell you later,' Marge mouthed back between 'Joy of heav'n to earth come down' and 'fix us in thy humble dwelling'.

Gordon was not himself. She had never seen him so morose, so listless, not even during his time at the town hall, and there had been plenty of those down the years.

The shaken fists, the angry phone calls, the screams in his face – he had learned to cope with abusive couples demanding that he push them up the waiting list for a house. But when Marge discovered that a woman had spat in his face, she told him it was time to think of quitting.

Marge prided herself on her generous nature. She understood the hopes and desperation of those seeking council accommodation. But she had seen what some of them did with their prize; had looked in horror at the broken windows, overgrown gardens, heaps of rubbish and scrap vehicles on the roadside on Darley Estate when Gordon had given her a tour one day from the safety of their Morris Marina.

As a school secretary, she had also seen what some of those tenants produced: grubby offspring who turned up hungry and tired from being left to their own devices while their work-shy parents boozed it up at the pub or spent their benefits on cigarettes and bingo.

No wonder, then, that Gordon had earned a reputation for being grumpy. He had laughed about his not-so-secret nickname but she knew it hurt. So, when they had let him go, as they put it, Marge had expected to see the old smile return. The redundancy money would give them a few nice holidays. She might even talk him into a cruise.

*

WHILE his wife was praising the Lord, Gordon was unshaven and in his pyjamas at 11am, doing a jigsaw and missing church by choice for only the second time in his life. He could not face the outside world.

It was the shock to the system of being finished so abruptly after all his years of service. That was what he had told Marge, at least. She must never know about the daughter he had secretly fathered, if indeed he had. The fact that Linda Barclay had no proof that the child was his was of little consolation. The mere suggestion was bad enough – and now Howard Wragg knew.

The director had assured him his secret was safe and, on that basis, Gordon had agreed to go quietly, though there was nothing to bind Wragg to his discretion, unlike the confidentiality agreement Gordon had had to sign, barring him from disclosing information about his work. Nor was there any guarantee that Barclay would keep her silence.

It was the uncertainty that unnerved him, that haunted his waking hours: the fear that what he had done would emerge, not through a front-page exposé in the *Bugle* – for surely, not even they would stoop so low – but from a whisper here or there, enough to draw knowing looks from friends at the bowls club or Round Table.

How could he live with the shame, let alone the ice that would descend on his marriage if the 'truth' came out? Marge was not the type to up and leave him. Keeping up appearances was in her blood. But he would lose her unyielding love and, just as painfully, her respect.

THE Rev Peter was one of a new breed of Church of England clergy, recruited in the hope of attracting younger worshippers to dwindling congregations.

Some of his innovations had not gone down well but the St Andrew's faithful had warmed to the introduction of tea and biscuits in the church hall after morning service and it was there that Marge quietly unburdened herself to her elderly friend.

'I can't understand why Gordon's taken it so badly, Geraldine. I mean, we know how things work at the town hall – the bigger earners are always first in the firing line when they're making cuts. And between you and I, we've done quite nicely out of it financially. I can't help thinking there's something he's not telling me.'

'Really?' said Geraldine, gossip antennae twitching. 'And you've no idea what it might be?'

'Not really. that's the annoying thing. Well – and I might be a million miles off the mark here – but he did once mention there'd been an "issue" over a company they were dealing with. Then he clammed up about it and when I asked him later, he got quite shirty.'

'I've got a shirty one at home,' Geraldine laughed. 'So, he didn't say what the "issue" was?'

'No, but I remember the name of the firm because it was unusual. Sewter Heating.'

'Mmm. Doesn't mean anything to me,' said Geraldine. 'I'll ask Nelson. He knows all sorts of people, with his Probus connections.'

'Just tell him to be discreet. Please, Geraldine. And Gordon mustn't know I've mentioned it.'

'Of course not, dear. Don't worry.'

'How is Nelson, by the way? And you? I'm so wrapped up in my little problems I've not even asked. How rude of me.'

'Don't be silly. We're fine, thanks. He's doing more "research".' She rolled her eyes. 'Thinks he might write another book.'

Marge chuckled. 'What's it about this time? He's done buses and railways, hasn't he?'

'Canals, dear. Says he wants to compile the definitive history of local canals. Hmm. I ask myself: is the world ready for this?'

*

STORIES fall into place in the unlikeliest of ways. Trails rich in promise turn suddenly cold. Missing links appear on the whim of a chance encounter or a million-to-one coincidence. The best stories come to nothing, while treasures stem from the flimsiest tip-offs.

It was a journalistic creed Simon knew well, yet there was not a hint of promise about the assignment that Colin had marked beside his name in the office diary.

His feelings were only of dismay and betrayal, his cheeks flushed from the row that had ended with the editor thumping his desk and ordering him to drop the story about Councillor Rose Sutton's philandering husband.

Simon was still smarting from the decision to relegate Frank Noon's expulsion from the Labour Party to an inside page. He could live with that, though. Politics was like Marmite to readers. But a council sex scandal was a rare gem.

He had accused the editor of lacking news sense, of burying a good story.

'What story?' Colin had snapped. 'That a bloke's being unfaithful? To who? Some nobody councillor? Who cares, mate? It's not as if we're in Victorian times. Besides, I'm getting fed up of hearing readers say we're becoming like *The Sun*. We're a traditional local rag, Simon. Remember that. You're my star man but I'd like to see you put more time and energy into positive, community stories.'

'Like what?'

'Like that canal book idea I've put you down for. And how about a series on the youth club scene? There are hundreds of people involved, you know – an audience of future readers we hardly ever reach.'

'Oh great! I bet that's never been done before. And there was I thinking I worked for a proper newspaper, not a parish magazine. To quote you, boss, it sounds as boring as tits without nipples.'

What annoyed him most was not having to drop the Rose Sutton story, but this honest-to-goodness reporting stuff.

He'd done more than his fair share of good-news stories. He had a degree in fruit and vegetable shows, for chrissake! But when big stories came along, the least he expected was a chance to tackle them. Colin could surely have made time for him to investigate, just by loading some of the routine work on to Gary Bostock. If ever there was a glory boy in need of more Sunday school anniversaries and church bazaars in his journalistic diet, it was the number two on the *Bugle's* reporting team.

'You off to see Mr Merryweather?' Gary smirked, seeing the thunder in his colleague's eyes.

'Bollocks!'

'He lives next door to your friend, Mrs Darlington, doesn't he?'

Simon ignored him.

'You could have a game of cards,' Gary chuckled.

'Sod off!'

Ninety-year-old Deidre Darlington was known to all at the *Bugle* as 'the Screaming Skull', her plummy voice audible across the newsroom whenever she phoned with news of the Guide Dogs for the Blind Association, and her hip replacement.

'Never know your luck,' Gary called as Simon skulked out, 'you might catch her and Merryweather at it. Playing cards, I mean.' But the afterthought came too late to stop a vision of Mrs Darlington being podgered on Nelson's antique sofa, surgical-stockinged legs akimbo, false teeth chattering like a privy door in a gale, orgasmic gurgles lifting paint off the window frames.

*

NELSON Merryweather was 79 but felt naughty as a nine-year-old.

He finished the dusting with a skip and a titter and put away his pinny. The anticipation was delicious.

He thumbed his case of cassette tapes, toying briefly with Louis Armstrong before settling on Nat King Cole. Snuggling with a squeak into his green leather armchair, he positioned the coffee table so that a plateful of Marks and Sparks rich fruit slices was in easy reach, then found his place in John Arlott's cricket column in *The Guardian* and pulled his favourite pipe from the pocket of his zip-up cardigan.

The very thought of a lusty romp with Deidre Darlington, or anyone else for that matter, would have locked Merryweather's knees in painful spasm. Arthritis was so much his jailer that even his monthly visits to Probus meetings were in doubt until the last minute.

As press officer for the club for retired professional gentlemen, he was responsible for submitting reports to the *Bugle*. 'Young Goodacre' always sent one of his reporters around to collect them and Merryweather had taken a shine to 'the boy Fox'.

Shame about the long hair, he thought, but he saw in Simon something of the incisive mind he himself had possessed as a young man. Merryweather enjoyed teasing him about typos and aberrant apostrophes, and their conversations would occasionally throw up snippets of gossip that he could use at Probus dinners.

Today, however, it would be Merryweather's turn to serve up a morsel. He could only hope the reporter's palate would appreciate its delicacy.

That Grebby business had upset him. He knew how close Geraldine and Marge had become. But mostly he had been intrigued. Sewter Heating: the name had rung a faint bell and he had soon combed through a contacts book, bulging with the fruits of 40 years in education and a decade on the magistrates' bench, and made a few calls.

He greeted Simon with a warm handshake, poured tea and told him to dig into the fruit slices. In no time, he had recited some biographical details and a few quotes to go with the article but, as Simon shuffled in his seat in readiness to leave, Merryweather steered the conversation around to his arthritis and the grim prospect of another winter in his bungalow.

'It's no good,' he said. 'Much as I love the old coal fire, I think I'm going to have to get some heating installed. But it's such an expense.'

Simon looked around a room stuffed with antiques. His heart bled.

'Oh, I can afford it,' Merryweather laughed. 'But if one's going to spend all that money, one wants a proper job doing. You wouldn't happen to know any reputable contractors, would you? I bet you hear things in your job.'

'None spring to mind,' Simon said, getting to his feet, 'but I'll have a think. Well, thanks for the interview and I hope the book comes off. Sorry, but I must be getting…'

'Of course you must, dear boy,' Merryweather said, reaching for the newspaper on the sideboard. It was the latest edition of the *Bugle*.

'This company's been recommended to me,' pointing to a single-column advert on a Classifieds page, 'Let us SEWTER you!' it read. 'Gas, electricity, oil, solid fuel… for all your heating needs, call the best, Sewter Heating. Telephone Brexham 2729.'

It was the sort of ad that appeared week after week and yet Simon had never noticed it. 'Right,' he said with a shrug, wondering if he should mention Eileen's pipes and whether the old man was fishing for something.

'I was talking to an old friend of mine at the town hall,' Merryweather said. 'Apparently, this company is carrying out a big contract for the council. I'd think that's a fair recommendation, wouldn't you? And I'm told their boss lives next door to the housing director, what's his name?'

'Howard Wragg?'

'That's the chap. Small world, isn't it?'

Merryweather peered over his spectacles for a flicker of emotion. There was none. He was impressed.

'Can't say I've heard of them,' Simon said nonchalantly, 'but I'll ask around.'

Merryweather watched him wend his way between the bee-buzzing lupins that stretched to the front gate, then went inside and roared with laughter.

5

SEWTER. Wragg. Director. Neighbours. Cover-up. Exposure. The words ricocheted around Simon's head.

He studied the minutes of the meeting that had awarded the contract to Sewter, just in case, during all the time he had scanned that sheet of beige paper, he had missed a note saying the director of housing and the company's owner were neighbours.

If Wragg had known of the connection – and how could he not have done? – and deliberately concealed it, was this a one-off? Or the sort of thing that went on all the time behind closed doors at the town hall?

He ached to get his teeth into the story but knew his editor well; knew he approached the task of filling his newspaper in the same way that he had been raised as a child: dinner first, then dessert.

And a Wednesday in a slow news week was no time to press his claim for hefty capital expenditure – ie, four quid for a search of Sewter's records at Companies House.

Time to butter up the boss, he thought, and set about writing a gushing piece about Nelson Merryweather's book.

Colin Goodacre could rarely be accused of being a clock-watcher but only an emergency would stop him getting away early for his weekly Scout meeting. He called the reporters into his office.

'Right, lads,' he said with a customary rub of the hands, 'this'll have to be quick but we're on the verge of a big story and I wanted to get everyone involved. As you know, Simon's had a tip-off that the housing director helped his neighbour win a council contract. So, what might we be looking at?'

'Corruption?' offered Roy Dunne, the office junior, rapidly growing in confidence.

'In what way?'

'Uhm, the director's taken a bribe?'

'Pfft!' muttered Gary Bostock 'That's got "libel" written all over it!'

'Gary's right, of course,' the editor said. 'We can't go accusing people of taking – or giving bribes – unless we can prove it beyond doubt, otherwise they'll sue the pants off us. Simon?'

'Well, you would think there's money been paid or favours done, wouldn't you? But Colin's hit the nail on the head with that word 'proof'. And all we can prove at the moment is that a contract was awarded to a firm on the advice of an officer who – apparently – lives next door to the firm's boss.'

'Apparently being the operative word,' smirked Gary.

'Yeah, apparently,' Simon bristled. 'But finding out where two blokes live is hardly the height of investigative journalism.'

'But what if they do live side by side?' Colin shrugged. 'They might both be completely unaware of the fact.'

'Yeah, right!' his chief reporter snorted. 'And the moon really is made of green cheese.'

'I'm playing devil's advocate, to a point,' the editor smiled, 'but we need to tread very carefully. We can't go *suggesting* anything. We can only write what we *know*. Facts, facts, facts, chaps!'

'And what we *know*,' Simon said, 'once we've established the addresses, is that Sewter got a lot of public money with the help of Wragg. We know it was on Wragg's recommendation that the sub-committee awarded the contract. That's a fact and I reckon our readers would be appalled by that, even if we can't prove any actual corruption.'

'What about the councillors?' asked Roy. 'Do you reckon they know and said nothing?'

'Perhaps they're in on it somehow,' said Gary. 'How many snouts are in the trough?'

'Dunno,' said Simon. 'They might all be bent for all we know. This could be the tip of the iceberg and they're taking backhanders left, right and centre. Who knows what might come out later? But for now…'

'Did they even know about the connection?' said Gary

'We don't know that either. All we can go on is what the official record says, and that's the sub-committee minutes. There's nothing in there about Wragg mentioning the connection or anybody raising it. As for councillors, nobody's talking, which doesn't prove anything. But we can mention that none of them are talking, can't we? Then readers can draw their own conclusions.'

'Good point,' said Colin. 'Right, this has been a useful discussion but here's how I see it: we can't use the C-word because we've no evidence of corruption. The best we can hope for is the D-word – dodgy. Has Wragg done something he shouldn't have done?'

Simon looked askance. 'You mean, is this sort of behaviour acceptable for someone in his position?'

'No, obviously not. But what exactly is his crime, if you will? Does the council have any rules governing contracts, for instance?'

'Do you mean standing orders, boss?' Roy chirped. 'We've just covered those at college.'

'Exactly, Roy. Well done. Get hold of a copy.'

*

BACK at his desk, Simon found a note asking him to call Lynne.

'Nothing to worry about, sweetheart,' she said immediately and went on to make him laugh with a long-winded tale of her visit to the post office to fetch the War Pension and how the new postmaster had refused to pay her, convinced she was on the fiddle with someone else's book, until a neighbour stepped in and explained the family's circumstances.

The knowledge that she was so good with money had allowed him to become blase about it. His father's death had started the process and his mother's had quickened it to the point where he would spend what he wished. If he felt like taking a taxi to a job, or fetching a takeaway or buying a new LP, then to hell with it!

He had also taken to telling friends that he did not expect to live beyond 40 and that anything more would be a bonus. He was not being morbid, he'd say, just realistic in view of his family history: all the more reason to believe that life's fruits were there to be plucked and savoured today, not risked on a tomorrow that might never come.

With Lynne behind him to pick up the pieces, he could afford such a cavalier attitude, but he knew he ought to tell her, just occasionally, how wonderful she was.

*

DETAILS of the company search arrived in the post four days later, confirming Ralph Sewter's address and major shareholding in Sewter Heating Ltd.

With 48 hours to deadline, Colin drove Simon and photographer Terry Minter to the leafy village of Horlton, three miles away. Wragg's address was recorded in the council's handbook and they quickly located his substantial detached house, separated from Sewter's bungalow by a neat garden and a picket fence.

Terry took pictures of both from the roadside, and an unexpected bonus: Sewter's face, full frontal, as he emerged casually from his front door. It matched his picture in a local magazine about upcoming businessmen and would sit nicely alongside one of the many shots of Wragg in the *Bugle*'s files.

The following morning, all three of the *Bugle*'s phone lines were busy. Simon was calling Sewter's office. Colin was asking Mavis Farnsworth if her husband could come to the phone. Gary was on to Wragg's secretary. They were closing the escape routes.

The background piece was already set in print, waiting for the 'nose' to be added. There was brief personal stuff about both men, details from Sewter's latest accounts and tales of cold living conditions from Eileen Clitheroe and a handful of other council tenants.

The editor had laid down the strategy. They would be direct with the key players, tell them straight what the paper knew and ask them to comment.

He left the calls as late as he dared, desperate to avoid the risk of news leaking out to other media. He had bitter experience of council spoilers. This time there would be no fudging press release designed to take the wind out of the *Bugle*'s sails.

Banking on all three targets being available at the same time was a gamble that could go horribly wrong. But, as Simon gave the thumbs-up, then Gary, Colin's shoulders relaxed.

Sewter was affable and talked freely, He had known 'Howard' as a neighbour for several years. Nice chap. Of course, he knew what he did for a living! And the contract? Yes, a coincidence, wasn't it? But that was all it was. He wanted to be clear about that. He was a respectable businessman. He had done everything properly and he was sure the council had, too.

Wragg was frosty. 'You know I can't comment on matters discussed by members in confidential session,' he said and hung up.

Farnsworth was dismissive. He would 'look into the allegation', he said, but he was sure there was no story, and frankly, he was surprised that the editor of the *Bugle* did not have better things to write about.

'That's good enough for me,' Colin said as the three swapped notes. 'Let's run it.' Then he enjoyed a rare treat: he rang the printers and told them to hold the front page.

Wragg and Farnsworth were Freemasons in the same lodge. Sewter belonged to another. This the journalists knew from a copy of the county's Masonic yearbook, which Frank Noon had somehow obtained and Simon had feverishly photocopied.

Such links could have led them to put two and two together and make five, especially given Colin's obsession with what he called left-handed bricklayers.

Simon typed the catchline in the top-left corner of a sheet of copy paper: *Exposed/1.*

'Just stick to the facts,' Colin kept saying, watching over the reporter's shoulder as words and phrases ping-ponged between them and pages torn out in frustration were hurled at the waste bin.

'What do we *know?*' the editor said. 'What can we *prove?*'

At last, they agreed on the intro: 'An inquiry was promised this week after it emerged that a top council officer helped his neighbour win a council contract for a heating system that went wrong.'

'Inquiry?' Gary frowned.

'Indeed!' said the editor. 'When the leader of the council promises to look into something, that's an inquiry as far as I'm concerned.'

Simon typed on. 'The *Bugle* can reveal that Brexham council's housing director, Howard Wragg, advised councillors to accept a £57,000 tender from Sewter Heating Ltd, whose managing director lives next door to him in the village of Horlton.

'Under the council's standing orders, councillors or paid officials with a personal connection to a company bidding for council work are required to declare an interest and take no part in the discussion. That did not happen in this case.'

The rest came easily but it was almost half an hour before Simon had typed 'ENDS' at the foot of the text and Colin had read, altered, re-read, altered again, re-read again and declared himself satisfied.

'Brilliant!' he beamed, and promptly wrote the headline:

COUNCIL HEATING

CONTRACT SCANDAL

Never before had he used the s-word so prominently in print, and when Gary suggested it might be a bit strong, the editor reached for his dictionary. '"Something likely to cause public outrage",' he quoted. 'I think I can safely say that if I went into the street and asked Joe Public what he thought of such behaviour, he'd say it was outrageous.'

'True,' said Gary. 'But you always tell us to stick to the facts and that headline seems a bit opinionated to me.'

'OK,' the editor said, trying not to look affronted. 'You got something better in mind?'

'How about,' Gary said, pulling up to Simon's desk and taking control of his typewriter:

HOUSING DIRECTOR

HELPED NEIGHBOUR

WIN COUNCIL DEAL

'Mmm,' the editor frowned and closed his eyes in contemplation. 'That's better,' he said at last, 'and it scans nicely. We'll go with that.'

He reached into his jacket pocket, pulled out a small brown tin marked 'Manikin', with a picture of Pegasus in one corner, lit a celebratory cigar and said, 'If that doesn't put some sales on this week, I'm a Dutchman!'

He was equally confident, however, that when readers in their thousands picked the *Bugle* off their doormats the next day, most would head straight for the Births, Deaths and Marriages columns.

*

KEN Farnsworth ended an uncomfortable phone call, put up the 'closed early' sign on the door of his greengrocer's shop and headed home.

He had thought it wise to consult the Labour Party's regional organiser. The response had been brutal: they could not afford another lingering scandal, not in the wake of the Tommy Jepson affair; not after some of the tabloids' gleeful Labour-bashing over Frank Noon's expulsion.

By the time J.H. Riddle's ancient press was spewing out copies of tomorrow's *Bugle*, Howard Wragg had arrived at the leader's home for tea, biscuits and an inevitable outcome.

The director had talked things over with his wife. He knew that a battle would be futile. It was all about the terms, and Farnsworth was in no mood to haggle. The leader realised that the alternative to an amicable parting was a disciplinary process, with all the public muck-raking that might entail.

'I'm so sorry it's come to this, Howard,' he said as the director rose to leave, 'but don't take it too badly. After all, who hasn't done a friend a favour occasionally?'

A friend? A favour? Huh! Something like that, Wragg chuckled sardonically on the way home. But the full story would never be told; not by him. It was too personal and, if his discretion led others to think worse of him, that was a price worth paying.

He remembered as if it were yesterday. A hot July afternoon. Friends and neighbours round for a barbecue. Howard not watching the children. Hearing screams. Running to the pond. Angela thrashing about, swallowing water. Ralph wading in. Ralph pulling her out, gasping but alive. Wragg would have given anything for the moment that saved his four-year-old daughter's life. No reward was ever sought or offered, never a hint of a debt that might one day be called in. But when his neighbour approached him in tears, driven to the verge of bankruptcy by the collapse of a major customer, Wragg needed little persuasion to help.

6

FARNSWORTH spent the next morning fielding calls from evening newspapers, radio and TV stations following up the *Bugle*'s story.

He called a press conference for four o'clock in the mayor's parlour. The press office sulkily failed to tell the *Bugle* about it but Frank Noon got to hear and phoned Simon. Colin went with him, keen to relive his reporting days.

They found themselves in a throng of microphones and cameras and elbows jostling for scribbling room. It was the sort of media circus usually reserved for news of royal visits.

Farnsworth faced the pack alone and read a prepared statement, 'The Personnel and Performance Sub-Committee has accepted a request by the director of housing that he be allowed to take early retirement on medical grounds.'

'Jeeez,' Simon muttered.

'I wish to make it clear,' Farnsworth continued, 'that this request was made some time ago and has no connection whatsoever with recent scurrilous press reports. Thank you, ladies and gentlemen. There will be no further comment.'

'Is he getting a pay-off?' shouted a man from the BBC, but Farnsworth was gone, leaving the reporters to chatter among themselves.

Simon turned, aghast, to his boss. 'What a whitewash!' he said. 'The bastard's got away with it. And this lot,' he nodded towards their media rivals, 'they're going to pick the story clean before we can have another shot at it. By the time we come out, people will have forgotten this is all down to our front page.'

'So,' the editor said, throwing an arm around his shoulder, 'we'll remind them next week. Besides, you got it first. That's real news – revelation, not reaction. Anyone can do a follow-up.'

And with that he extended a furtive foot, sending the BBC man tumbling into a painted lady from the Local Government Journal.

Outside, Frank Noon was handing out copies of his own statement. 'I will be asking the district auditor to investigate the award of the Sewter Heating contract,' it read. 'I will also propose a vote of no confidence in Councillor Farnsworth at the next full council meeting.

'I regret to say that this episode shames the Labour Party, of which I was once so proud.'

*

WRAGG'S departure was only a minor victory as far as Frank was concerned. He ached to hurt the council leader. All he needed was proof that Farnsworth knew of the contract scandal and covered it up.

He could think of only one man who might talk, though the strained relations they had endured gave him little hope of success as he caught a bus to a Wimpey estate on the outskirts of town and knocked on the door of a prim semi.

Gordon Grebby greeted him just as he had expected, with a familiar curl of the lips that passed for a smile and a terse refusal to discuss anything to do with the council. Frank tried all his charm, promising he would do nothing to blacken Grebby's name; insisting that all he wanted was to establish what role councillors had played in the affair.

'Please,' Grebby said as he closed the door, 'leave me in peace.'

In the month since his enforced retirement, Grebby had found himself almost incapable of thinking straight. Now, as he watched the receding figure of Frank Noon from his curtain peephole, a thought struck him; one that disturbed yet thrilled him, striking at the heart of a core belief but offering hope of an escape from the chains of his guilt and anxiety.

No sin was graver than lying. That lesson had been drilled into him by God-fearing parents. But age and experience had taught him that there were greater lies and lesser lies.

He dialled Wragg's home number.

'Gordon!' his old boss sounded pleased. 'How's the easy life suiting you?'

'It has its ups and downs,' Grebby replied, finding that first untruth surprisingly easy. 'As you're discovering, I gather.'

'I'm sorry to hear how things worked out for you, Howard. I know we didn't always see eye to eye but I think you tried your best in difficult circumstances and I'm sure there was nothing malicious in that Sewter business. Incidentally, I hope you realise I had nothing to do with the press finding out.'

'I didn't think that for a moment, old chap,' Wragg lied. 'And I appreciate your kind comments. Truth is, I was stupid and I've paid the price for it. You did your best to warn me but I didn't listen.'

'Actually,' Grebby said, voice lowered as if someone might overhear, 'I wanted to warn you that Councillor Noon's been sniffing about. Would you believe it – he turned up at my front door?'

'Good heavens!' Wragg was genuinely surprised. 'What's he after?'

'"Confirmation" was how he put it.' The lies were coming more easily now. 'He said he knew I'd tried to talk you into declaring your interest, though he can't possibly have known that. He's a devious so-and-so but I've grown wise to his little tricks.'

'I'm sure you have,' Wragg purred.

'He even claimed Councillor Farnsworth knew all about it and covered it up. I gave him short shrift, of course, but he asked me to get in touch if I ever wanted to discuss it. I told him absolutely nothing and I won't. You have my word on that.'

'That's much appreciated, Gordon,' Wragg said, already thumbing his phone book for Farnsworth's number.

'Oh, and Howard,' Grebby added, 'that business of mine? You did promise, didn't you?'

'I did indeed and I shall honour that promise,' Wragg said. 'In fact, I can't even remember the lady's name.'

*

WRAGG'S phone call to Farnsworth set in motion a train of events that would lead to Frank Noon's testicles.

The prospect of further press coverage did not worry the disgraced director personally. His reputation was shot to pieces already. A show of concern for

Farnsworth's might serve him well, though, since Wragg's severance pay had been authorised but had yet to appear in his bank account.

Farnsworth thanked him for the warning. It was good to know he could count on Grebby. Frank Noon was another matter entirely. The council leader knew that one careless remark by his former comrade could bring him down, and Noon had a habit of using council chamber privilege to say things he could not substantiate and would not dare repeat outside.

It was at times like this that Farnsworth was grateful for friends in the police. One in particular was not averse to making use of criminal associates. The director picked up the phone.

*

NO great powers of detection were required to establish the whereabouts of Frank Noon on a Friday evening.

Barring an emergency council meeting, he would be at the Black Swan with his reporter friend.

Tonight was different only in that a figure was watching from the shadows across the road as Frank entered the tap room.

The councillor scowled at the sight of Simon standing in a corner, eyes fixed on a screen, body twitching as he moved a lever with one hand and a dial with the other, resulting in a series of 'booms' and 'pings'.

'Wasting your money again, I see,' Frank huffed as he sidled up to the machine, pint of bitter in hand. 'Destroyer, eh?' he said, spotting the name emblazoned above the screen of this newfangled arcade game. 'These damned things'll destroy the pub trade, I reckon.'

'Stop being an old fart,' Simon laughed as a spindly image of a submarine sank and the screen turned blank.

'Things change, mate. I bet your dad's generation thought the world would end when they put jukeboxes in pubs. Besides, the landlord gets a cut of the takings, so perhaps these things'll be a lifeline.'

The conversation soon turned to familiar ground. The press conference had made local radio and TV as well as the evening papers. There was even a snippet in the *Daily Telegraph*.

'It was good to get rid of Wragg,' Frank said. 'I blame him partly for Tommy's death, you know. He could have intervened when Grebby refused to give the old lad a new place. He could have spared Tommy that damned trial. Pity Farnsworth came out of it smelling of roses, though.'

'Well,' said Simon, 'you can't win 'em all. We got rid of one bad apple and there must be others for you to expose.'

'True,' Frank smiled, wondering briefly if he should mention his visit to Grebby but thinking better of it.

He stayed behind when Simon left but was ready for his bed after downing three more pints and being badgered by an old couple about broken paving slabs on the street outside their bungalow.

He did not see the skinny figure watching from a bus shelter as he began his wobbly walk home.

The watcher waited until he had rounded a corner, then padded after him. He saw him turn into a jitty and set off to outflank him on Doc Marten tiptoes, cutting through gardens, down one street and up another, reaching the jitty's end with heaves and pants so loud he was sure his prey would hear him. There he waited.

The footsteps grew louder. He pulled on a balaclava and lifted a foot, steadying himself against a garden fence. A glimpse of the councillor's face, then he let go, smiling as it hit something soft.

Frank doubled up with a groan. A knee met his falling face and his nose burst. The figure grabbed him by the ponytail and yanked the bloodied face towards his own.

'Listen, grandad,' he snarled into Frank's pleading eyes, 'just keep yer fuckin' nose out o' things wot don't concern yer. Or next time yer'll be dead.'

He raked up a mouthful of phlegm, spat it in Frank's face, then turned and ran.

7

THEY buried Fred Bains with his wife, toasted him with tea and sandwiches at Woolworth's restaurant and headed home from Hull in Lynne's trusty old VW Beetle, immersed in the balm of childhood memories.

Squeezed into the back seats, Paul and Dawn laughed as Simon recalled how Fred had stuck up for him when he'd he spilt his mad professor's jam jar full of water and dead flies on Grandma's best tablecloth.

They remembered Grandad returning from solo shopping trips, loaded with best ham and huge cream cakes and insisting to his stony-faced wife that he had not called at the bookies.

This First World War veteran, survivor of the Somme, was the biggest, gentlest, funniest man they had ever known and they pictured his miner's knobbly knuckles, the veins that stood proud on his forearms, the thick shock of white hair that never seemed to thin and the little point on top of one ear.

They remembered him in his black suit, dressed for Sunday lunchtime at the British Legion club; how he'd come home in even better humour to demolish a vast plateful of dinner topped with pork crackling and a wedge of Grandma's suet pudding, then disappear for his 40 winks, leaving the kids to wonder if all old people winked as they slept.

They talked of dreamy school holidays at the grandparents' house, where no one nagged them about their manners and they could stay up late, sipping stout from Grandad's pewter tankard and gorging on chocolate biscuits.

He taught them how to play rummy and took them to see the pit ponies at the colliery where he spent his working life. He let them climb on top of his shed and jump off when Grandma wasn't looking. Cometh the ice-cream van, his hand went instinctively to his pocket.

He let them fart without pardon me-ing and never allowed his own giggle-wrenching explosions to pass without declaring, 'Wherever thou be, let thy wind go free. In church or chapel, let the bugger rattle.'

Now he was gone, and Dawn sensed that the end of one era was a good time to herald the start of another.

Over dinner that evening, she said, 'I've got something to tell you all. I'm going to join the RAF.'

'We'll see,' Simon said. 'One day, perhaps. A lot can happen in two years.'

'I'm not waiting two years,' Dawn said calmly. 'I can start in four months, soon as I'm 16.'

'Don't be silly,' he said, 'You've got school to finish first. And like it or not, sis, you've got to live by my rules for a little while yet.'

It was the first time he had spoken to her like that since their mother's death; the first time he had felt the need. He regretted it at once and fixed her with a stare, the sort that had once made her wilt. She stared back, eyes blazing defiance.

He had hardly noticed that she was growing into a beautiful young woman, with her mother's high cheekbones and even the small bump in her nose.

'Anyway,' she said, 'I've done the theory test – and passed. I just need to get my O-levels and then I'll take the physical. All being well, they'll take me on as a trainee airwoman. I'd probably do my training in Lincoln. Or there's a centre in Norfolk.'

'Norfolk?' Simon spluttered, casting a quizzical glance at Lynne and meeting an it's-news-to-me shrug. 'But that's the other side of the world!'

'Typical journalist, always exaggerating!' Dawn laughed. 'It's not that far. And I'd come home every month or so to start with.'

'So, when did all this happen?'

'Last month, when I was staying with Aunt Dorothy. I'm sorry, Si, and,' she paused for breath, 'I still need your permission.'

'But why all the secrecy? I thought we were closer than that, sis.'

'We are, and I was going to tell you. But you seemed so busy at work and Lynne's doing such a good job running the house and being a second mum and I wanted to do something for myself for once. Haven't you always said "don't wait for tomorrow"? Since Mum died, I can see that more than ever.'

She sounded so grown-up, and he looked at the gravy going cold on his plate. Had he been such a failure as a guardian that his kid sister felt the need to escape at the earliest opportunity? He could refuse permission, of course, but that might drive a wedge between them for ever.

Nothing had prepared him for this.

'What about school?'

'What? Stay on and waste two more years for a few stupid A-levels? And then what? No thanks! I want to see a bit of life while I can.'

'But what about us? It won't be the same without you – even if you are a pain in the bum at times. We've just got settled again.'

'You'll cope!' she said, squeezing his forearm and flashing her wide smile, the one he brushed for her when she was little. 'You two'll always cope.'

CHAPTER THREE

1

COLIN Goodacre's death was fittingly newsworthy. And past deadline.

Driving back from a meet-the-bosses lunch at Tyler's Steelworks, he found himself behind a Tyler's lorry loaded with girders and wondered if they formed one of the new orders the company had just announced.

The lorry braked sharply at traffic lights and a rope tied carelessly around its load gave way. Half a ton of steel slid off the flat-bed trailer. One crashed through the windscreen of the car behind and pierced the editor's chest like a skewer through rice paper.

Since it happened on a Friday, other local news outlets were able to run the story long before his own paper. Typical, he would have said.

The funeral ten days later filled the Methodist church where Colin had been an assistant Scout leader.

The great and the good of Brexham turned out to pay their respects. Scouts formed a guard of honour as the coffin was carried inside by pallbearers headed by Colin's cousin Maurice. Councillor Frank Noon wore a tie. Annie Shaw had a new hat. Even Detective Inspector Jim Richardson was there, having travelled all the way from Whitby, ostensibly for the occasion but primarily to spend a night with Flick Beresford's sister.

Taking notes for a report of the proceedings helped Simon to endure them with an air of detachment. It was only when the family filed out and he glimpsed the face of Colin's youngest, a girl younger than his own sister, that a lump formed defiantly in his throat.

*

HE had never harboured ambitions to be an editor but life had a way of making big decisions for him and, when Walter Harding, eyeing early retirement and with no appetite for change, offered him a choice between filling Colin's shoes or obedience to an unknown quantity from outside, Simon accepted a modest pay rise and a company car – a brown Nissan Cherry, the fruits of a deal between Walter and a newly opened showroom with money to spend on advertising.

After years spent waiting for buses and traipsing the streets, he now had free transport and a desk job. His appointment as one of the country's youngest editors made a paragraph in the trade press.

Responsibility was no stranger to him but power was a new and seductive beast and his career enjoyed an adrenalin rush. Decisions came easily. No more passing the buck over what was published. No more bleating 'I'm only the monkey'. He was now the organ grinder.

But old habits die hard. People were his passion and he figured there was no point having power if he could not pursue that passion. So, on a fine Saturday morning, when he might have relaxed at home and sent one of his juniors to cover the job, he set off for the League of Friends' annual bazaar in the grounds of Norton General Hospital

His thirst for recording the minutiae of local life was as strong as ever as he toured the stalls and games, noting who was doing what.

The Girl Guides had a bran tub raising money for a special wheelchair for one of their number. The Scouts' smash-a-plate stall was in aid of new headquarters. The Townswomen's Guild president's granddaughter presented a buttonhole to the VIP opener.

It was all utterly predictable until he bumped into Jenny Worthington, one of the blue-rinse set from the Conservative Ladies' Coffee Club.

'Just the man!' she said, unusually bold. 'Could I have a quiet word, Mr Fox?'

Jenny had been out canvassing for new recruits to the Tory party and had come across a sad story, she said, adding, as if sensing the editor's cynicism, that it had nothing to do with politics.

A resident had told her she was sick with worry about her granddaughter. Eight-year-old Daniella, who lived in Poland, was seriously ill with a brain tumour and the operation she needed was not available in her homeland.

"His grandma wondered if the good people of Brexham might help her raise the money to bring the girl to England for surgery," Jenny gushed.

'Do you think it's something the *Bugle* might be able to help with? It took some persuading but I brought the lady with me today. I thought someone from the *Bugle* might be here.'

She turned towards the tombola stall and stretched out an arm. 'Krys! Come over here, darling.'

The bony figure looked as if it had once belonged to a tall, handsome woman but now wore grubby clothes, an apologetic stoop and a face that had forgotten how to smile. It struck a chord at once but he was thrown by the setting. Then it hit him, and he needed every ounce of control to stifle a guffaw.

Krystyna Tatham was a star turn at Brexham Magistrates' Court. Having fled Poland shortly after the war, she had in recent years taken to wandering drunkenly on to local railway lines, for which she was repeatedly hauled before the Beak, only to weep and plead for forgiveness from 'you lovely English people'.

We'll see how lovely they are now, he thought, as he guided the old soak to a seat and found a clean page in his notebook.

*

SIMON'S phone call to Poland that evening produced the flesh required for the bones of Krystyna's story.

He found her daughter Nadia refreshingly calm and clear after that tearful interview. Daniella, she said, had first complained of headaches more than a year ago. They gradually became worse and more frequent. Then she began vomiting regularly and having blurred vision.

'It seems so unfair,' Nadia said, her voice cracking. 'She's always been so busy and active. She'd just started playing netball and loved it. But now she's scared of pushing herself in case she gets ill.'

Months of tests and visits had led to a diagnosis: a tumour called a meningioma was pressing on Daniella's brain. The tumour was benign and only in very rare cases did such growths become life-threatening. But in any case, her health would continue to deteriorate as the tumour grew.

'We've been told that surgery is the only answer,' her mother continued. 'Trouble is, it's in a really awkward place, apparently – trust our little monkey! –

and the surgeons here say it's too risky to operate.

'There's man in England, though, they all speak very highly of, a Mr Topham. They say he's one of the best in the world. He's seen the scan results and thinks he might be able to help.

'It's expensive, though – at least £10,000 – and we don't have that sort of money. But we'd never have dreamt of asking people in England for help. It was mum's idea. I'm so proud of her.'

'Leave it with me,' Simon said at last, relieved to give his note-taking hand a rest and remove the telephone receiver wedged between neck and shoulder. 'We'll do a big story in the newspaper and see what happens.'

*

TWO days before deadline, two photographs arrived at the Bugle office by fax from Poland. One showed Daniella in her prime. The other portrayed a pale, thin girl with sallow eyes. Their graininess somehow added to their impact when positioned side by side under the headline 'YOUR HELP COULD SAVE THIS GIRL'S LIFE'.

Krystyna had been too ashamed of her appearance to be photographed – 'she'll come round soon', Nadia had insisted – but her emotional appeal was sure to tug at heartstrings, ending with the words: 'Please don't let my precious girl die'.

By mere coincidence, the story dominated the front page on the same day that a short piece inside told of a flasher on the banks of the Morbury Canal.

The police description of the man the paper dubbed 'a pervert in pyjamas' could have applied to any number of Brexham's young men: well-built, 6ft 3in, black hair, aged 25 to 30, tattooed forearms.

If the constabulary had not been so coy, it might have added 'towering muscleman, manic grin, mad staring eyes, two gold teeth, hung like a horse' and half the town would have known it meant Wagga, the police included. But arresting Dean Wagstaff was not a task to be undertaken lightly.

'Filthy pig lies!' Krystyna would snarl whenever she read of Dean's antics in the press. They could say what they liked. He was a good boy to his Aunt Krystyna: hot-headed at times but that was the Slav in him.

He had been her lodger for two years now, since she had heard about him living rough. She had taken him in and enjoyed his company, as well as the security of having a man about the house. The neighbourhood brats with their door-knocking and stone-throwing didn't come now.

Dean was handy around the house, too, and, odd times when his aunt's resolve to forget the past was washed away by cheap sherry and she cried through drink, then drank to stop the tears as she thought of her Nadia, settled in the old country with her Polish husband and little Daniella, it was Dean who found her in the early hours, stone-cold on the kitchen floor, who eased the bottle from her hand and carried her to bed.

He was a generous boy, handing over most of his dole money and asking only that there was food in the pantry.

Krystyna was happy to believe that he did some labouring work on the side to earn beer money. Wagga thought it best not to mention the uppers and downers he sold in pubs or swapped for TVs or bikes carted off by a new breed of young and prolific burglar; or the boyfriend trouble he'd sort out for a night's drinking.

It would have broken her heart.

Besides, she was good insurance for when he got nicked. He'd tell Probation how he was looking after his confused, alcoholic aunt, how he was all she had, and the magistrates would usually let him off with a slapped wrist.

If he could have eavesdropped on their deliberations, he would have learned that they cared less about Dean Wagstaff and his aunt and more about public safety. After all, why bang him up at huge expense for a few months of training in the prison gym, honing that fearful physique for its next assault on society?

2

SIMON pushed open the heavily varnished door to what years of drunken scratching at its glass panel now heralded the 'Pub ic Bar' of the Three Feathers, and brushed past an elderly figure hunched over a copy of the *Bugle*.

'Much in it this week, young man?' he asked.

The old-timer's face emerged with a toothless grin beneath a Guinness-foam moustache. 'I dunna bother about th'articles,' he said in a coal-dust rasp. 'I just gerrit for t'deaths column. T'mek sure I'm still 'ere!'

They laughed in hearty union, though the editor had lost count of the times he had heard that line.

In celebration of a small rise in circulation, he was treating the staff of the *Bugle* to lunch. All but Walter Harding. The MD preferred to have his potted meat sandwiches and slice of pork pie at his desk.

The Feathers' usual fare of cheese or meat cobs had been enhanced by the arrival of a modern marvel, a microwave oven, to the evident delight of receptionist Katie Tummins as she bit gingerly into a hot sausage roll.

'You know,' Simon beamed, nodding towards the old-timer with his Guinness, 'it doesn't matter how often I see that sight – someone with their head buried in the paper on a Friday – I still get a buzz. And the Daniella campaign has been a real tonic.'

He threw an arm around Gary Bostock, who had been hurriedly promoted to senior reporter after Colin's death, in the hope of staving off an early bid to lure him away to an evening paper. Successive *Bugle* editors had witnessed the depressing pattern, spending three or four years knocking rough diamonds into shape, only for bigger fish to come hunting, with salaries and expense accounts the local rag could not hope to match.

'We done all rate, ain't we?' Gary smiled, fond of mocking the local tongue in his posh southern accent.

'It's grabbed people's attention like nothing I've known,' Simon said. 'Just shows, there's no one like Brexham folk for generosity, and they've taken that kid to their hearts. It doesn't matter that her grandma's not exactly a pillar of the community…'

'Pillock more like,' Gary laughed.

'…or that the girl lives a thousand miles away. In fact, I think those two those things make it more appealing. They're all reading about Daniella and thinking, "What if she were my kid and all I needed to save her was money?" It's good to see people believing they can actually achieve something.'

In truth, it was not about lifting spirits. Operation Daniella had made filling the paper easier. For several weeks, the *Bugle* had been able to run stories and pictures about readers raising money for the fund.

The manager of Fine Fare had spent six hours in a bath of custard in return for donations.

WPC Wendy Marshall and two police colleagues had completed a sponsored walk.

Workers at Carrier's condom factory had turned into vicars and tarts for a fancy-dress pub crawl.

Members of the Royal Antediluvian Order of Buffaloes had staged a 24-hour pool marathon, spending more on beer than they attracted in donations.

And the landlord of the Unicorn Inn had beaten allcomers in a pickled-egg-eating contest by downing 14 in half an hour, for which he paid with a week of constipation.

*

LYNNE was stretched out on a towel and sun-kissed to the brink of sleep when Simon arrived home, padded silently across the lawn and blasted her with a hosepipe. She screamed and cursed after him, wrestling him to the ground and covering his damp suit with specks of grass before pinning his shoulders down with her thighs. 'You swine!" she panted. "I was enjoying that.'

God, how he loved her!

She was the gentlest, prettiest, funniest, sexiest, most wondrous thing he had ever encountered.

They had been soulmates from their first date. Both were 15 and he the envy of his school friends. But it was much more than the firm breasts – large for a girl her size – the pert bottom that filled her faded Levi's to perfection, the hazel eyes, the full lips that burst back over perfect teeth as she laughed, that snared him for ever in her web.

She was so *real*. Just like him.

They wore the trappings of their generation, said the right things to please the herd, while despising the posing and posturing of adolescence.

Both ached for deep friendship and found it in each other's heads. Never had conversation been so bold and meaningful. Never had the frontiers of understanding been pushed so far forward, never so many truths revealed, never so many hilarities enjoyed.

She told friends she felt safe with him, knew he would protect her. But he was the vulnerable one. He had the big ideas but she the wherewithal. She kept her feet on the ground and held his down while his head was in the clouds.

There were smiles wherever she went, her outgoing manner the ideal foil for his innate shyness.

Throughout the turmoil of recent years, she had been there for him, and, for all his deep-down steel, for all his determination to keep the family together, he knew he would have been lost without her.

He thought of telling her this as she sat astride him on the lawn. Instead, his hand found the dampness of her bikini briefs.

'Someone'll see us!' she said.

'Give us a kiss then.'

He pulled her lips to his and ate her gasp as he pushed the flimsy cloth aside and eased a finger into her. She bit his ear and whispered, 'Let's go inside.'

Their knee-trembler against the kitchen sink was cut short by the slamming of the front door. Lynne dashed to the bathroom, knickers in hand. Simon, trousers around ankles, scurried sideways for the stairs.

'Sorry,' Paul smirked when they re-emerged as if nothing had happened. 'I'd do my flies up if I were you, bruv.'

It was dinner-at-the-table day, a twice-weekly routine that Lynne had insisted on when she moved in, and once Dawn had returned from netball practice, Simon had just enough time to consume fish fingers, chips and mushy peas before driving to the social club at Tyler's, where six beefy blokes were set for battle in a sponsored cow pie-eating contest. For Daniella.

*

HELPING a child in danger was all very laudable but Simon yearned for more. He sensed a story with wider appeal, if only Krystyna would talk.

He knocked several times at her front door, without response, then peered through dingy lace curtains for signs of life.

Until recently, Krystyna had been nothing more than a figure of fun to *Bugle* readers and a source of irritation to the criminal justice system. But what, he wondered, had brought her to this stage in life?

He knew she had come to England shortly after the war but what of the years before then? And how had she built a new life in a strange land?

He wanted to get under her skin.

He took out the note he had typed at the office, just in case, and slipped it through the letterbox:

'Dear Mrs Tatham, I wondered if you'd mind talking to me about your life, for a feature in the newspaper. I'm sure many of our readers would love to read about Krystyna, the woman, not just the grandmother of Daniella. I thought it might help the fundraising campaign as well. Perhaps I could buy you lunch sometime and we could have a chat. Please let me know.'

Inside, Krystyna waited until she was sure the caller had gone, then emerged from the gloom of her kitchen. She never answered the door.

She read the note and chuckled. 'Huh? He want know about me? What to tell? Some things best forget.'

Trying to forget was something she had spent much of her life doing. But now, as she closed her eyes and rested her head in her favourite chair, the one Dean had someone managed to afford for her at Christmas, a picture of Marcin flickered in her brain. Dear Marcin. Whatever would she have done without him?

Her eldest brother had emigrated to England shortly before the outbreak of war, having found work as a research scientist. Somehow, miraculously, he had traced her after liberation and paid for her passage to Southampton. With her brother's help and a smattering of English, Krystyna had found accommodation with a group of other emigres and landed a job as a waitress in British Home Stores.

It was while serving at tables in the store's busy restaurant that she caught the eye of British sailor Donald Tatham.

A whirlwind romance followed, culminating in marriage and, seven months later, the birth of daughter Nadia: evidence of pre-marital activity still considered shameful at the time.

They doted on the girl and family life was blissful.

Nadia was just 14 when Donald died in a car crash while returning home on leave.

Despite the huge hole in her life, the teenager grew into a bright and confident young woman as the bond between mother and daughter grew ever stronger.

It was partly the sense of loss that inspired Nadia to embark on what she called a voyage to discover her roots and so, in the summer of 1970, she gave up her bank clerk's job and travelled to Poland, intending to spend a couple of months exploring her mother's homeland and hoping to trace distant relatives.

Nadia had no intention of finding love but it found her and by the time she returned home, she had married a handsome engineer named Piotr.

Krystyna begged her to return to the UK but Nadia had her mother's iron will and foresaw a brighter future for the newlyweds and the children they hoped to raise in Poland.

Despite his skills, Piotr earned barely enough to support them once baby Daniella arrived, certainly not enough to travel regularly to England

Letters and photos arrived regularly from Poland but, in eight years, she had seen her granddaughter only once in the flesh, when Nadia brought her to England shortly after her first birthday.

Krystyna's life had gone from full to empty. It was not, however, the loss of her beloved Donald, nor the fact that she could not hold and kiss her granddaughter, that began her spiral into drink and depression. The answer lay in a five-digit number tattooed on her left forearm, signifying: prisoner of Auschwitz.

More than 30 years on, the memories of that place were still so painful, so ghastly, that she could not bear to speak of them, yet they haunted her dreams, ever more so without a loving husband and daughter to fill her waking hours.

Nadia had asked her many times about the camp and the fate of her grandparents. Krystyna would say only that they had been separated from her when the train loaded with Poles from the Łódź ghetto arrived at Auschwitz. She would never see them again.

How could she tell her daughter what had happened there? How all but a few of the endless stream of those who jumped or fell from the suffocating carriages had promptly disappeared? How they had been marched off to so-called shower blocks, only to be gassed to death in screaming, choking huddles of young and old before being speared with pitchforks and fed into furnaces?

How could she tell her child of the straw beds on which she had slept fitfully, crammed against other skeletal figures; of the floors awash with diarrhoea and vomit; of the shootings and lynchings; of the smell of burning human flesh that hung over the camp with the crematoria in full flow; of the gold teeth she had been ordered to pull from piles of bones that were once beloved fathers, mothers, brothers; of how she debased herself to please her captors, just so that she might live another hour?

These were not things a mother should share with a daughter. They belonged to another world, one that deserved to be buried, not dignified with recollections.

Besides, deep down, Krystyna felt guilty for being alive.

3

FRANK Noon left the town hall in triumphant mood after persuading a meeting of the council to make a £100 donation to the Daniella fund. Dumped by Labour, distrusted by the Tories, the sole Independent had led them by the nose and guaranteed himself some favourable publicity in the process, though it could hardly have been easier. After all, who wanted to appear a skinflint when a young life was at stake?

He called at the miners' welfare on his way home. There, too, humble folk were raising money for a little girl they had never met, but Frank left after a pint of brown ale, thinking he'd heard better sounds from a distressed cat than from some of the singers in the talent show.

As he bent to peer over safety fencing beside the rapidly expanding gully along the route of the Town Traffic Corridor, he winced: a reminder of his frailty since he was beaten up in a dark alley ten months earlier, by whom and for what reason he knew not.

That the attack happened days after Howard Wragg's early retirement over the Sewter affair had struck him as more than coincidental. The attacker had told him to keep his nose out of 'things wot don't concern yer', but that hardly narrowed the field: Frank had poked his nose into many dark corners over the years.

The bruises had healed in time but, every now and then, a sudden movement would trigger a stitch-like pain that he presumed was linked to that kick in the testicles.

The police had told him their investigation remained active, whatever that meant. The *Bugle* had carried appeals for witnesses. But, short of the culprit turning up at the police station to confess, Frank had given up hope of anyone being caught. Hardly surprising, he realised, since the only description he was able to give was that of a skinny man wearing a balaclava. And the voice: hoarse and breathy.

He stared at the road cutting, 40ft deep in places, and sighed.

Pinder Terrace was now just a memory. The last houses had been demolished within months of Tommy Jepson's death and once the money had been allocated, Frank's former Labour allies had signalled full steam ahead.

He shook his head at the sight of Denham Place, glinting in the moonlight on the far side of the cutting.

Frank had tracked the fate of those 12 terrace houses in three blocks for years. Condemned under the original scheme, the family homes had been spared when the plans changed, then put back on the market, but at a knock-down price, reflecting the fact that they would one day be sitting on the edge of a major road.

Given first refusal, the former owners had snapped them up and proceeded to split them into bedsits, filling them with tenants who could not afford to be choosy – alkies, druggies and ex-cons – and whose rent was guaranteed by the DHSS.

How much public money had found its way into the hands of property speculators as a result of lines being drawn and redrawn on a map? The cynic in Frank wondered if it had all been staged from the start.

But that was all in the past. Nothing could stop the road now.

Contractors were hard at work. Dozens of lorries came and went daily, transporting huge heaps of spoil to building sites near and far.

Before long, Brexham would be one more monument to the motor car, while those who had stood in its way tried to forge new lives in unfamiliar surroundings on out-of-town estates.

So many hopes dashed, so much misery endured. A community had been cut in two and his beloved town would never be the same again.

4

KRYSTYNA laid the *Bugle* on the floor beside her bed and reached for the brass-framed photo of her granddaughter on the small table where she soaked her teeth.

'So many good people,' she sighed. 'Me, I don't deserve nothing. But you' – she put the frame to her lips – 'you, my precious, you come to Babcia. Babcia make it better.'

Three days had passed since her last drink. This time, there would be no clinics, no counselling. This time, she promised herself, she would do it on her own because if she could not pull herself together for Daniella, she did not deserve all those good people, and without them, she might never see her again, and then she would be no better than a dog and should be put down.

Each Friday fuelled her new purpose. She would buy two copies of the *Bugle*, cut out articles about Daniella from one and paste them into a scrapbook. The other she posted to Nadia, who read it avidly and passed it to her local paper in Poznań, whose own coverage of the campaign brought pledges from readers towards the family's air fare.

The *Bugle*'s fund had topped £7,000, over halfway, but time was running out. Daniella would soon be too sick to travel.

Krystyna wanted, needed to do something to help. But what could she do, an old drunk? She tossed and turned in bed. Her mind, unable to sink into the blackness to which the booze had so often led her, whirled with the thread of ideas that were swept away by feelings of hopelessness as soon as they arose.

She had turned her back on the outside world for so long that she no longer knew how to communicate with it. She lacked the skills to write letters to businesses and charities, seeking donations. She had no friends of wealth or influence. She could not sing or ride a bicycle or swim a sponsored mile or do a mountain hike.

She could not sleep for thinking, and sleeplessness robbed her of the ability to think clearly. An arm reached for the bottle beneath her bed and a cold sweat broke on her brow as a fleeting image of Daniella appeared, her face gaunt.

She knew not when it came but sleep enveloped her at last and when the yapping of next door's dog stirred her shortly after 6am, she sat up with a broad smile.

'Paska!' she gasped. 'I make the best paska ever!'

She hurried to Dean's room but found his bed undisturbed and muttered that it was time he found himself a nice girl instead of whoring all night.

On any other day she would have sulked in rejection. But now a thought crept upon her and she shuddered with fear: she must tell someone else about her plan, and that meant reaching out beyond the confines of a life which had for so long been sour and secretive.

The thought of putting on a show for the world outside was so alien that she hardly knew where to begin but at last she hoisted her grimy nightie around her waist and washed roughly with a flannel at the bathroom sink.

In a cupboard beneath the stairs, she tore at a box of clothes left contemptuously untouched since some 'busybodies' from the Sally Army had delivered it months ago. Though creased and musty, they were the only garments she possessed that were neither stained by food or sherry or stiff with weeks of wear.

Like a girl dressing her favourite doll, she tried on each one, pulling faces of horror and delight in front of the wardrobe mirror, finally settling on a blue Crimplene trouser suit and a red and white polka-dot blouse.

She rummaged in the bathroom cabinet for the face compact Dean had bought for her birthday. There was no sign of it but she found a blue and yellow tin with the words 'Mycil foot powder'.

'Foot, face,' she chuckled, 'what the effing 'ell!'

Sprinkling the white powder on to a wad of toilet paper, she dabbed at her mottled cheeks and stubbly chin until her face was white as an angel's, then rubbed a handful of her nephew's aftershave behind her neck and ears and stepped out into a sultry Sunday morning.

As Krystyna passed what had briefly been Tommy Jepson's home, his daughter Jean was almost apoplectic with mirth. 'What the...?'

Krystyna sensed the curtains twitch and could not give a damn. For once, she would not reward the neighbours with a two-fingered salute or a mouthful of Polish abuse.

A shaft of light had entered her world, so bright that it pierced the aching misery that had cloaked her all these years.

All she could think as she walked, head up, towards the church, stomach held in to stop the blouse gaping between strained buttons, hand tugging at the trousers that rode up into the crease of her backside, exposing several inches of flesh above her ankles, was: paska, paska, paska!

A familiar shortcut took her past a children's playground. She glimpsed a scrawny figure standing nearby and turned the other way, anxious not to engage with the 'little skinnyhead' she had seen many times outside her back door, whispering with Dean as money and packages changed hands.

*

FLICK Beresford pressed his face against the bow-top iron railings surrounding the playground of his childhood, eyes fixed on a little girl squealing 'higher, Mummy, higher' on a creaking swing.

'Look, Mummy,' she yelled as the swing came to a halt, 'it's Uncle Shane.'

Flick grinned and waved. He longed to hold her.

Tracey shot him a half-smile, for Lucy's sake, then bundled the girl into her arms and headed for the gate, resisting her pleas to stay and play.

'We've got to go shopping, sweetheart,' she said as Lucy peered over her mother's shoulder and pulled a face at the funny gap-toothed figure with his dog on a rope.

'But I could stay here with Uncle Shane.'

'Not today,' Tracey said, parp-parping the girl's nose with a squeeze that made her giggle.

'Not any day if she has her way,' Flick muttered. 'Selfish cow!'

He had been doing a lot of thinking.

So, what he had done was wrong, in the eyes of the law at least. But he had been off his face that night. And anyway, would it hurt to let him spend a little time with Lucy? She was just a little girl. She didn't know where she had come from.

It was not as if he would hurt her and even if he had to be plain Uncle Shane, for now, he could live with that. One day, perhaps, Lucy would find out the truth and then, well, she would either forgive him or hate him to his last breath.

Besides, he figured, brothers and sisters, mothers and sons, fathers and daughters had been screwing each other since man had a hole in his arse. Look at the aristocracy.

Mum and daughter were holding hands, walking one moment, skipping the next, and Tracey felt the stress slipping from her shoulders as the distance between them and her brother grew. He made her flesh crawl, and his presence was all the harder to bear now that she was growing in confidence, and nervousness at the same time.

Confident because she had finally given her policeman lover the push and was free of the stifling secrecy that had cloaked her since his arrival in her life.

Nervous because Lucy was growing up fast and asking awkward questions, like: why was Uncle Shane never present at family get-togethers?

Without Jim Richardson in the background, knowing as he did what had happened between brother and sister, she feared that her brother might feel emboldened to get closer to her. She would not have put it past him to blurt out his secret in a drunken moment. He would probably even blame her.

It was not enough to tell herself that she had done nothing wrong, that she was not the one who should feel ashamed. The fact was that she did, and she feared that the longer she kept the secret, the more she gave it some sort of respectability. If the truth were to come out now, seven years on, some might think she had hidden it because she was guilty.

Either way, how could Lucy live a normal life?

Flick watched them fade into the distance. He had seen more of Tracey about town of late. Did that mean Richardson was out of the picture? If he could only be sure, he would knock on her door and ask her straight out if he could see his daughter now and again. But what if they were still together and she told Richo? The officer might have a word in the wrong ear and, rough as Flick's mates might be, they had no time for paedos.

Tugging his whippet to heel, he headed for the Unicorn with a reassuring tap on the rear pocket of his Wranglers. Inside was a small plastic bag of amphetamine that he had cut with baking powder, just enough to give him a few snorts' profit when he met up with the usual Sunday lunchtime crowd of groundworkers and scaffolders, ever keen to crown the weekend with a little chemical assistance.

Tracey, meanwhile, was contemplating an adventure. The PR firm where she worked was expanding. There was talk of a new role on the East Coast, not far from Auntie Val. It would mean promotion, a new challenge, more money and a fresh start, away from Brexham, where everybody knew her name.

She knew, though, that being so far away from Lucy would break her mum's heart, and vice versa. How could she justify her own happiness over the knowledge that the two people dearest to her would suffer through no fault of their own?

*

PASTOR Jeremy Heathcote was a small, wiry man with gentle eyes and a warm smile that belied the fire with which he preached the gospel. So passionate were his sermons that hard men in the congregation had fallen to their knees, scorched by the sweet and cleansing embrace of the Holy Spirit.

He spoke today of the eighth commandment: thou shalt not steal. To his knowledge, a quarter of his congregation had convictions for shoplifting.

The Evangelical Assembly was a church as much of the sinner as of the sinned against and its minister was well-groomed in reaching out to those who had fallen by the wayside. His previous calling as an insurance salesman had taken him into homes where children suffered abuse, squalor or cold indifference. Was it any wonder that some turned out the way they did?

Today, having made his customary appeal to the flock to show their neighbours an act of love, he felt the Lord would allow him a glow of satisfaction at the sight of Mick Prestwick hugging a stranger in their midst, one so clearly bewildered by it all.

Dear Mick. Such a blessing to the church, so loyal and hardworking and yet so gentle: the same Mick who had once broken a shop girl's nose with a head-butt when challenged over stealing a bottle of brandy; the same Mick whose dalliance with drugs had led him ever downward until he was injecting whisky to get high; the same Mick whose life had been changed for ever by a vision of Christ outside a chip shop.

It was Mick who introduced the pastor to his neighbour during tea and biscuits after the service. The minister could recognise a product of hard knocks at 50 paces but there was something in this woman's eyes, a spark of hope that captivated him. He worked hard to get her talking and the words at first stumbled out nervously, then came in torrents as Krystyna chatted through welling eyes about her granddaughter.

By the time he waved her goodbye, the pastor had written the church hall phone number on a slip of paper and slid it into her handbag, telling her not to hesitate if ever she needed help. He had also committed the church to raising money for Daniella – a party with barbecue, perhaps, and folk music or gospel songs. But on one condition: Krystyna must be there, with paska by the plateful.

*

THE air in Pearl Shooter's hairdressing salon was thick with peroxide and indignation.

'Never again!' screeched an old dear from beneath a dryer. 'Bought it since I were married, I 'ave, but never again.'

'Jesus!' Detective Inspector Jim Richardson muttered at his desk at Divisional Headquarters, Whitby, when a copy of the *Bugle* article arrived by fax from his old nick. 'They ought to rename it the *Scumbag Bugle*.'

In the playground of Brexham Comprehensive, a gaggle of schoolgirls pored over a picture of the sort of young men their mums warned them about, and debated who'd they like to 'do it' with.

The phone on Simon's desk was white-hot.

'If I have to listen to one more bloody complaint about that picture...' he growled.

He felt like telling the lot of them to stick the paper where the sun didn't shine. Bad men doing good things was news, for heaven's sake! If he kept people out of the paper just because they'd misbehaved at some point in the past, it would be half-empty.

Instead, he was calm and polite, telling each caller who would listen that he was glad they had taken the trouble to ring, rather than seethe in silence, and he was sorry if the article offended them but it was a newspaper's job to reflect all aspects of local life and he was sure that if they looked at it overall, week to week, they'd find it mirrored local events fairly and reasonably and...

'Up yours too!' he snapped as yet another cut him off.

The outcry was over his front-page exclusive. Below 'MUSCLE FOR DANIELLA' the sub-heading read 'Hard men go soft to help heart girl' beside a grinning line-up of known criminals and troublemakers who were planning a sponsored lorry-pull up High Street.

Wagga had set up the interview in the bar of the Unicorn, having talked 13 fellow testosterone dummies into helping his Aunt Krystyna.

Simon had spent an hour squeezed between this mountain of machismo, his armpits sodden, thinking: they could 'disappear' me as easily as the KGB. A few flexed pecs and stamped feet and I'd be mashed into a puree and they could drink down every last drop and no one would ever know.

The likes of Jed Hall, who had done time for throwing his girlfriend into a bath of scalding water, oozed one-liners about helping a poor, defenceless kid just like their own – and, along the way, confessed to a litany of past sins that would make a valuable addition to the *Bugle*'s archives.

The editor now had all their pictures on file, just waiting for the next time one of them appeared in court.

*

IN his nine months at the helm, Simon had grown used to fashioning a front page from the best of a mediocre bunch of stories – polishing a turd, as Colin would say – and so the knowledge that there was a cast-iron splash on the way was a blessing indeed.

A local businessman had been in touch to pledge the last £2,000 needed for Daniella's operation. It was an opportunity for the paper to celebrate people power: ordinary folk making the difference between life and death.

Like most residents of Darley Estate, Krystyna did not have a phone, but Tommy Jepson's daughter Jean did and when Simon called her with the news, she hurried to tell her neighbour.

Krystyna felt fit to burst. She hurried off to see Pastor Heathcote, whose first reaction was to cancel his fundraising party. It was still three weeks away but the singers and musicians had started rehearsing, the food was on order and the VIP invitations had gone out.

Krystyna pleaded with him to go ahead. It would be a thank-you party for all the wonderful people who had helped her, she said, and instead of selling her Polish delicacy for 10p a slice, she would serve it up for free: her little way of giving something back.

5

DANIELLA was admitted to an isolation ward at Great Ormond Street Hospital within hours of the family's arrival at Heathrow Airport. Surgeon Peter Topham wanted several days to assess her in person and consider detailed scans before deciding whether to go ahead.

Come the morning of the party, Krystyna shopped furiously. She had found her mother's recipe on a slip of paper between the pages of a Bible she had rooted out from a long-abandoned trunk.

It was surely a sign.

Her emotions were laid raw by the warmth of shop assistants who greeted the transformation from notorious wino to local celebrity with open-mouthed astonishment and sent her on her way with free margarine and eggs and best wishes for her granddaughter.

Her excitement grew with each purchase and she almost ran the last few hundred yards home for fear of exploding with laughter or peeing herself in the street.

Inside, she collapsed breathless against the door. Now she would make the best paska ever.

But, as she looked at a sink piled high with dirty pots, with the party less than eight hours away, her knees went weak at the enormity of the task and her mind turned to the bottle beneath the bed. She stamped her foot to drive the thought away. It was no good: she would have to abandon the paska.

IF he was honest with himself, Pastor Jeremy savoured the prospect of good publicity for the Living Church almost as much as the thought of helping Krystyna in her good deed. Two local radio stations had promised to be at the party. The BBC might send TV cameras and the *Bugle* was bound to come.

'And what's wrong with that?' he wondered aloud between checks on the salad and sandwich fillings.

'Talking to yersen now, are you?' The pastor turned to see the oversized teeth of his loyal convert Mick Prestwick in a huge smiled.

The clergyman's cheeks flushed. 'Ha, Mick! You caught me at it. It's my age you know. How's it coming along?'

Mick brought a cleaver down on another chicken, tossing the legs into one large metal tray and the breasts into another.

'Everything's under control, minister,' he said. 'This is going to be one hell of a barbecue,' he added with a grin towards the heavens, 'No offence, your honour.'

The pastor moved on, checking that all lots for the charity auction were present and correct but hurried to answer when the church hall phone rang.

'Don't worry, love,' he said. 'Calm down and we'll sort things out. I know just the person to give you a hand.'

Within an hour, he had driven to Darley Estate, collected Krystyna and her bag of ingredients and delivered her to the door of a smart little flat in Bewley Terrace, where a pint-sized pensioner opened the door.

'Nice to meet you, darlin'!' beamed Annie Shaw. 'Now, come inside and let's 'ave a look at this recipe o' yours.'

For what seemed an age, the pair of them beat and mixed and stirred and kneaded to create the sticky Easter bread that Krystyna's mother had baked on special days back home. And when it was all turned out and Annie's kitchen was like a furnace from the oven and their exertions, Krystyna demonstrated how to drizzle it with icing before sprinkling on candied fruits, chocolate drops, chopped nuts and sugar strands.

Then they carved it into strips and stacked them in every tin and Tupperware pot Annie possessed.

*

THE drive from Whitby was quicker than expected and Jim Richardson had an hour to kill before meeting up with the crew from his old nick for farewell drinks with retiring superintendent Bob Clegg, then a taxi into the city for a curry.

It was two months since his last visit to Brexham, since the break-up with Tracey. It was her call and he had offered little resistance. She deserved better than long-distance hook-ups when he could get away and, in any case, he was running out of excuses back home.

They had parted on good terms but it would be awkward if he bumped into her now. More chance of coming across her reprobate brother, he figured. Not a prospect he relished. But, as he ambled around his old stomping ground, there was no sign of Flick or his regular crew.

He noticed the same poster in two shop windows before curiosity got the better of him and he stopped at the third. It was headed 'Help for Daniella'. Below a picture of a young girl, it read, 'Please join Mrs Krystyna Tatham for a party to celebrate the successful conclusion of a campaign to raise money to bring her granddaughter to England for life-saving surgery. Everyone welcome!'

'Good god!' Richardson chuckled.

He knew her notorious side, of course; had met her as she sobered up in the cells after her late-night wanderings on to the rail lines; had even got her off with a caution instead of a charge occasionally, something that had enabled him to lever useful information from her grateful nephew Dean Wagstaff.

But Krystyna the celebrity, the party host? Truth sure was stranger than fiction.

Richardson read on. The party was at the Evangelical Assembly that very evening, ten minutes and a few hundred yards away.

*

THE church hall was filling up rapidly as Krystyna and Annie arrived. Pastor Jerry greeted Krystyna like the prodigal returned and she blushed at his booming announcement that the lady who had made this all possible had joined them.

She felt like the Queen holding court. People she had never met greeted her with handshakes and congratulations. The mayor was there in his chain. Cameras flashed. Reporters buzzed around, asking questions.

Simon was feeling uneasy. There was always the danger on occasions like this that a rival reporter would beat him to a better angle. He had seen it before:

cultivating contacts during a long-running story, doing all the right things, representing them honestly, pointing out the pitfalls of saying this or that, helping them to look better than they perhaps deserved, only for them to go gooey-eyed when faced with a TV reporter they had never met – because the camera never lied! – and blurt out something they had never told him, and suddenly he had been scooped on his own doorstep.

*

FLICK swallowed a tiny purple disc, wrapped five more in a Rizla and left Stu Miller's house with a promise to pay once he had sold the rest.

'Go steady, man, it's far-out stuff,' the dealer laughed in his broad Scottish brogue.

If there was one thing that Flick's extensive knowledge of recreational drugs had taught him, it was that LSD was far-out.

He called at Fine Fare on his walk through the town centre and headed for the booze display. Making no attempt to hide it, he stuffed a bottle of Newcastle Brown Ale into one pocket of his Crombie, then loitered at the liquor shelves before marching boldly towards a familiar store detective.

''Ere, darlin', he smirked, pulling out the beer, 'I were only kiddin'. I'm goin' straight – honest! In fact, I'm just off to church.'

The guard watched with incredulity, blissfully unaware of the stolen quarter-bottle of whisky in Flick's other pocket.

The acid was kicking in and he had not eaten all day. He figured there was bound to be food at the party for that sick kid.

Wagga had warned him to stay away. He still had the hump over a speed deal. Sure, Flick had ripped him off, but Wagga couldn't prove it. That was enough, though, for him to ban Flick from the sponsored lorry-pull, so while all his mates were looking good with their pictures in the paper, he had missed out.

Anyway, he thought, bollocks to Wagga. The old lady had said it was a party for all the good people of Brexham, and Flick figured that, in his own way, he was one of the best.

*

KRYSTYNA bristled as she caught sight of her nephew, evidently in some sort of confrontation with his skinhead friend.

Pastor Jeremy sensed trouble and hurried as discreetly as he could to the door, where Wagga was telling Flick he could not come in. The minister thanked his volunteer doorman for doing an excellent job but reminded him of his aunt's wish. Wagga relented with a shrug of his huge frame.

Flick was soon buffeting one cluster of guests after another en route to the buffet, oblivious of the evil eyes.

The acid was in full flow.

Cymbals crashed and lights exploded in his head. Faces with grossly disgorged lips slurped from melting cups held by rubbery arms. He heard a horse whinny and spun around to see a skeletal face below a beehive perm, its jaws chattering in demonic laughter beside a man with a pig's head.

'Fuck me!' he muttered. 'I need a drink.'

Pastor Jeremy was on the stage with an announcement: a reporter from the BBC – bastard!, thought Simon – had arranged for Peter Topham to be on the phone from from Great Ormond Street Hospital at that very moment. The brief call ended with the news that Daniella's operation would go ahead within the next few days. Cheers and cries of 'praise the Lord' echoed around the hall.

Flick found a wall to lean against in the hope of stemming the hysteria coursing through his veins. He pulled out the whisky and glugged voraciously at the searing liquid until it had nowhere to go but back out, gushing down his chin and the front of his T-shirt.

Standing a few yards away, local GP Dr 'Joe' Chowdhury was enjoying a joke with Councillor Noon when he happened to glance in Flick's direction.

'Oi, Paki! What yer laughin' at?'

The hall fell quiet. In one corner, DI Richardson stood on tiptoe, braced to intervene.

Flick pushed his way towards the GP, pointing a grubby finger.

Frank Noon froze. That voice! He knew it at once. It was the same hoarse, breathy growl that had threatened to kill him as he was beaten up in a dark alley almost a year ago.

'Sorry, old chap.' The cool bedside manner for which Dr Joe was renowned had deserted him and he spluttered in a voice that sensed danger, 'I was just…'

Flick's forehead smashed into the bridge of the doctor's nose, strangling the sentence in a burst of crimson.

Wagga arrived seconds too late to prevent the impact but grabbed Flick by the neck as his head recoiled, and hauled him towards the door.

Inside, the hush gave way to gasps, then screams, then a hubbub of people rushing to help the wounded GP.

Outside, the sole of Wagga's trainer sent Flick stumbling half-upright across the uneven lawn towards the smouldering barbecue, his face stretched wide in horror, dilated pupils glinting from the hot coals on the trolley drawing ever closer.

Somehow, he summoned the composure to jam one leg down hard, halting the momentum for a second, but in doing so twisted an ankle and lurched forward again.

Inside, Pastor Jeremy was phoning for an ambulance for Dr Joe.

Outside, Flick's forearms felt the heat first. He shrieked and tried to pull them clear but his weight upended the trolley. His knees buckled and, as he fell back, coals and grilles cascaded after him in a cloud of ash.

As he tore at the scorching debris on his chest and screamed in a voice that made not a sound, one defiant ember found the whisky stain and sent a path of flame racing towards his neck.

Wagga walked calmly back inside, closing the door against the smell of human steak.

6

SIX DAYS later, with Daniella out of intensive care, Simon boarded a train to London with Krystyna and Pastor Jeremy.

In the Co-op carrier bag that served as his briefcase were a shorthand notebook, a camera borrowed from *Bugle* photographer Terry Minton and a cheque for £1,500, left over from the operation fund and destined for Great Ormond Street.

'Just point and shoot, you can't go wrong,' Terry had told him on handing over the Olympus Trip after managing director Walter Harding refused to pay for two staff to travel to London.

Other news outlets would have the story soon enough but Krystyna had promised that her first meeting with Daniella since the op would be a *Bugle* exclusive.

She was barely recognisable from the scraggy figure Simon had seen in court. Her hair was done up in a bun – by Annie, she explained – and her beige Marks and Sparks two-piece suit was a gift from the church.

She spent the journey with her face against the carriage window, transfixed as scenes of industrial decay and lush countryside flashed by, but could not contain her excitement during the taxi ride from St Pancras, breathlessly telling the cabbie, 'This my first time in London!'

They waited in Reception for only a few minutes before a tall silver-haired man in a smart suit appeared. 'Peter Topham,' he said, smiling broadly as he proffered a hand, then pinking slightly as Krystyna pulled it to her lips, gushing, 'God bless you, sir. You're an angel.'

The camera clicked.

'We're just pleased that we could help,' the surgeon said. 'I'm happy to say that the operation was a success and Daniella should be fit to leave us tomorrow, though we won't half miss her. The staff have really taken to her, you know. She's such a happy little girl, despite all she's gone through.'

He led them along a succession of corridors before pausing outside a small room and holding open the doors.

Sitting up in bed, looking strong and healthy, was Daniella, flanked by her parents.

'Oh, my gorgeous girl!' Krystyna blubbed, rushing to embrace her. And, for what seemed an age, all they did was look into each other's eyes.

Click, click, click.

Pastor Jeremy had booked a night at a hotel for himself and Krystyna. Tomorrow, Daniella would travel with them to Brexham, where Nadia and Piotr planned to spend a few days exploring the area and meeting some of the people who had saved their son's life.

Simon headed for the evening train home. His team had worked hard to fill the paper before his trip. All that remained was a large hole at the top of the front page, perfect for his picture of that bedside reunion, and the headline 'LOST FOR WORDS'.

CHAPTER FOUR

1

THE Richardsons had settled well on the North Yorkshire coast. The sale of their semi and 12 Pinder Terrace had paid for an old stone cottage overlooking farm fields two miles out of Whitby beside a quiet footpath to the harbour.

Eunice took up bowls and amateur dramatics. Jim rediscovered golf and kept his dick in his pants, outside – and largely inside –his marriage but had an eye on a pretty young sergeant at the station.

Clive Pullman was right about there being a better class of villain up there: Richardson's first major success was to bust a gang stealing tractors to sell for parts abroad. It made him an overnight hero in the farming community.

Then he discovered something that shocked him to the core: Eunice had been playing away. The faithful wife, his 'dried-up old prune', had been at it behind his back, and worse still with his boss, the smooth, oh-so-caring Superintendent Pullman.

The fact that he had not for one moment suspected what she was up to angered him all the more. She would never have got away with it in Brexham, where his ear was closer to the ground, and it was only when he returned early from a conference that Pullman had sent him to that he caught them at it, on his bed.

Eunice was hysterical. Didn't know what had come over her, she said. Begged for forgiveness. Promised to end it straight away. Said they could try again.

Not a chance, he said.

And Pullman, his old mucker, shrivelled into a corner as Richardson made to thump him, then thought better of it. 'I'm so sorry, mate,' his boss kept saying. 'Please, let's keep this between ourselves, or I'll be finished.'

Give me time, he said. I'll make things right.

You'd bloody better, Richardson said when they met later. Otherwise, he snarled, it was not just the chief constable he'd tell, but the press.

Two months later, he was heading back to his old stomping ground. Pullman had had a word with someone high up. Richardson didn't know who and didn't care: they were all on the Square.

There was a vacancy for the role of divisional head of CID for Brexham and its neighbouring borough and he was invited to apply.

The interview was a formality, he had been told, but he took no chances, presenting a paper on the drug scene and his plans to tackle it. 'It's something I'm genuinely passionate about,' he told the panel. 'But I often feel I'm swimming against the tide.'

2

FOR the first year after Colin Goodacre's death, life at the *Bugle* continued much as it had under his reign.

Simon thrived on the challenge of setting the news agenda and seeing it through. Then, a new era came out of the blue. Four suits descended on the office one Friday morning and announced that the *Bugle* was theirs, the latest in a long line of acquisitions by Horizon News Ltd.

No longer would it struggle for survival as a small, solitary ship in turbulent waters, they said. It had joined a corporate armada, sailing into a bright future.

The end of a century of independence brought mixed news for the journalists.

Plastic replaced hot-metal pages, computers replaced manual typewriters and the *Bugle's* own staff found themselves, not a set of hired printers, in charge of every word. If they typed it, that was how it appeared in print.

With control came a heavy burden. Before Horizon's arrival, every word in the paper was read five times before publication – by reporter, editor, typesetter, proofreader and editor again. Now, only the editor stood between what a reporter in a hurry typed with two fingers, and a potential libel. And breathing down the editor's neck as deadlines neared was Harry Barkes, Horizon's bumptious production director.

Barkes presided over a nationwide stable of weekly titles that were slick in appearance but thin on content and the pound signs in his eyes were clear from the moment he set foot in the *Bugle's* old-fashioned premises.

'Believe it or not,' he beamed as he led a stream of visitors around the newsroom with a flourish of a sausage-fingered hand and an air of disdain, 'these folks input every bit of editorial – even sport reports.'

Direct inputting by reporters replaced Linotype operators casting lines of print in hot metal, which meant lower production costs and higher dividends for Horizon's shareholders.

That the old setup was dying on its feet had been obvious to even the casual observer. It was only a question of time before bigger fish got their hands on the *Bugle*, and when Horizon came knocking, the sole surviving heir of the family that had owned it since its inception needed little persuasion to sell.

*

READERS began to sense something different about their weekly paper, though most could not pinpoint it.

Little had changed about the content. The pages, however, looked cleaner, the text and images sharper. Horizon had introduced heavier newsprint and printing had been transferred to the group's modern press in Nottingham.

The takeover spelled disaster for the company that had printed the paper for almost 80 years. The *Bugle* had long been Riddle's main source of income and the firm's antiquated flatbed press was suitable for little else. Income from commercial jobs such as flyers and posters, produced on an assortment of hand-operated linocut devices, barely covered costs.

Worst of all, the sole Linotype machine, with its vast array of brass matrices and its pot of molten lead, was mothballed overnight. It was a magnificent piece of engineering but no longer had a purpose. Dennis Riddle, the fourth generation of his family to run the firm, longed to see it in a museum but, since it weighed three tons and would have to be disassembled and rebuilt in minute detail, the only realistic course was to sell it for scrap.

Old skills, too, were destined for the scrapheap. Typesetter Reg Witham had spent 30 years learning and perfecting his trade. He was among the first five redundancies to be declared in the company's history.

Sad as it was to see anyone lose their job, the journalists had little sympathy for Reg and his print union pals, who had maintained a stranglehold on the newspaper industry, with their refusal to change working practices and their excessive wage demands, routinely earning twice as much for printing the news as the journalists who wrote it.

Just like the *Bugle's* family owners, Riddle's had sat on its laurels for decades, lacking ambition and investment. Now, the modern world had arrived.

*

FOR Frank Noon, too, a new era had dawned - and he was on a mission to tidy up his scruffy flat.

As he unplugged the vacuum cleaner, he contemplated his new role and thought that nothing summed up the pantomime nature of local politics quite like his first major engagement as mayor of Brexham.

In eight days' time, he would be welcoming the Rt Hon Norman Fowler, minister for transport, to officially open the Brexham Town Traffic Corridor.

'Me, of all people! How bloody ironic, eh, Dad?' he said, dusting a photograph that hung on the wall above the fireplace. He chuckled at the image of his short-trousered self on his father's knee, Then, suddenly, he began to dance, hips jiggling, arms pumping as he burst into song to the tune of a hit by the Clash:

I fought the road and the road won!
I fought the road and the road won!

And with that he slumped on to the settee, giggling until he coughed and spluttered.

'Aye,' he muttered, once his breath returned, 'I fought the bugger, I lost the battle and now I'm going to be shaking hands with a Tory toff and saying how good it is. You couldn't make it up.'

What made this particular town hall panto so farcical was that it was thanks to the party that had kicked him out for opposing the road that he had been elected as the borough's first Independent mayor.

Tradition demanded that he be given the role. He was, after all, the council's longest-serving member. But, given all that had gone before, Frank had resigned himself to Labour picking one of their own. And, as he discovered from his few remaining friends inside the party, that would have been the case but for the intervention of Tommy Jepson's daughter.

Jean Palethorpe had steadily grown in confidence during her two years as a councillor and had apparently convinced her colleagues that letting tradition take its course would give them the moral high ground, whereas abandoning it would cast them as spiteful and selfish.

Of that, at least, Frank mused, her dad would have been proud, though he could not help wondering if Jean had acted purely out of goodness or whether she, too, had heard rumours that the Tories were thinking of nominating Frank themselves, thereby turning the normally dignified mayor-making ceremony into an unseemly political squabble.

The diehard socialist was no fan of pomp and ceremony but knew the people of Brexham, knew they held the mayoralty in high regard, and since someone had to fill it, why not him? True, he might feel guilty about wearing a gold chain worth more than most of his constituents earned in a year. But he trusted himself to do his best for them. He would be a man-of-the-people mayor, still enjoying a pint or two, still playing dominoes at the welfare, still giving council officers hell over rotting window frames and mouldy walls.

Some things had to change, though. Carrying a cassette recorder in a rucksack slung over his shoulders was hardly fitting for the borough's 'first citizen' and he had baulked at the thought of resorting to notebook and pen to log the complaints he picked up on his travels. He was spared by the arrival in his life of a piece of technical wizardry; something that fitted in his pocket and meant he could still listen to reggae on the move.

The Sony Walkman was an extravagant gift from the woman he had chosen as his lady mayoress after several years of close friendship, though, on her insistence, 'no hanky-panky': Annie Shaw.

There was one other condition on which the spunky pensioner had agreed to take on the role: Frank's ponytail would have to go.

*

BACK in the age of independence, *Bugle* staff had harboured a sense of pride and purpose that made up for the poor wages and archaic conditions.

In Horizonworld, the journalists still believed that stories happened outside their four walls but found themselves increasingly desk-bound, anchored by the pressures of producing bigger papers as a hungry market grasped the fresh advances of pushy advertising reps. More adverts meant more pages. More pages meant ever-higher advertising targets set by faceless men in London, which meant more pages.

Managing director Walter Harding was reduced to little more than an office manager and when Gary Bostock, having lingered longer than most after passing his exams, finally joined the *Evening Gazette*, Head Office decreed that he should not be replaced.

At a stroke, the news-gathering team was cut by a quarter and another advertising rep was taken on instead.

The editor was blunt with his new bosses. They could talk all they liked about corporate strength and shared resources, he said, but the simple fact was that fewer reporters meant fewer stories of local interest.

He risked the wrath of Barkes by going over his head with a passionate letter to the group's managing director, explaining that court coverage would have to be cut, so the fire chief's wife on a shoplifting charge, for instance, might escape publicity because the editor could not afford a reporter hanging around all morning for a two-paragraph adjournment. With fewer bodies to cover council meetings, elected members might feel tempted to betray election promises, knowing that their constituents would be none the wiser.

Road accidents, fires and robberies would be covered less often or in less depth, he warned.

And which carnival or church fete would miss out with only one reporter on weekend duty instead of two?

Then there were the little things that meant so much to little people, things that gave them a moment in the sun: the champion cabbage growers and sponge bakers at the village show; the wedding couples and Sunday school soloists; the pigeon fanciers and whippet racers; the stars of darts, dominoes, table tennis, tenpin bowling and more – all tiny pieces in the jigsaw of community life that was the essence of the local rag.

With fewer reporters to process all those hand-written or ill-typed reports, submitted by readers themselves, some might fail to make the newspaper, and then people might give up submitting them, triggering a vicious circle of weaker content leading to falling sales leading to weaker content.

But even the prospect of lost revenue failed to sway the Horizon board.

Simon, with his long hair and liberal views, and Walter, with his cardigans and dribbling pipe, were now united against a common enemy: the bean counters who simply didn't *get it*.

Work nibbled ever more greedily into lunchtimes, evenings and weekends, but no longer for the sake of a better angle, a broader mix of news or more adventurous page designs. It was mere story shale to fill holes. Spirits sank.

For Simon, life at home had changed, too. Dawn had completed her training and shared a house in Norfolk with two other RAF girls. Sport-mad Paul had gained a place at university, studying architecture, of all things, and lived on campus in Leicester.

Peggy Fox's old, cold, rambling house had been too big for the four of them, let alone two, and even with their War Pension and two wages, the couple could not afford the renovations that inevitably lay ahead.

Besides, Dawn and Paul were due a third of Peggy's estate and the sale of the old place gave them £3,000 each, enough for Simon and Lynne to put a 50% deposit on a two-up, two-down closer to the *Bugle* office.

Home ownership was not something they had bargained for in the hot flush of their teenage idealism, in the days when they argued that property was theft; that the state should provide work, housing and all the basic amenities for everyone. In the days before reality kicked in.

Once again, though, circumstance had forced their hand. But they revelled in the challenge of decorating and furnishing a home of their own, and there they drifted into semi-detached respectability on pot, sharing an ounce of the drug occasionally with a handful of friends, all of them otherwise-upstanding citizens; all homeowners in steady jobs; all living in fear of their secret hobby being made public, bizarre as it seemed to them that consumption of a herb should trouble the justice system when it harmed no one but themselves.

The parties of old had given way to the odd spliff in front of the telly after work.

Simon's marriage had endured while more conventional relationships had collapsed around him. Lynne's eyes still flickered with the old magic but the premature burden of family life had etched her face with weariness.

One day, he swore, he'd take her away from it all; sell the house, put some money aside to start again and blow the rest on six months in the sun. He'd wrap her in silk and set her skipping through petal groves and white sands, miles from all the hassle, away from the clocks and car fumes, away from people with a story to tell who pestered them in pubs and shops.

They'd bathe in peace and solitude, in dazzling sunsets and sweet, fresh air, where home was a shack with no TV, where no one knew their names and they could be themselves, living on their love and their wits, before it was too late to be carefree again.

One day.

3

THE editor swivelled in his leather chair and cupped his face in his hands in an effort to quell the gnawing toothache that had come upon him in the night. It never ceased to amaze him that scientists could send men to the moon but had not devised a better means of chewing food than bits of bone that cracked and crumbled and caused agony. He made a mental note to write a piece about it one day.

It was August, the silly season for news. Schools and factories were closed, council meetings suspended and PR types were churning out press releases normally destined for newsroom bins, knowing that journalists would seize on morsels in times of famine: the pages had to be filled somehow.

But the weekend had brought news of a tragedy of rare magnitude in a small town. Two 17-year-old shop girls from the same estate had been killed when the taxi taking them home from a party smashed into a minibus full of firemen returning from a training camp.

Trainee reporter Diane Pickering picked up the story on her weekend calls and phoned her editor at home.

'It would happen at a weekend,' he said at once, and he could almost hear Colin Goodacre saying the same, except that he would have done it with a theatrical flourish and a speech about overpaid Fleet Street hacks feasting on the brutal facts while the poor old weekly papers grubbed around for a new angle days after the event.

The lack of urgency to get something into print did have one big advantage, though: when grieving relatives had calmed down from slamming the door on a stream of give-it-to-me-now reporters with daily deadlines, they made easy pickings for a sweet girl from the friendly local rag.

Just three months into her job, Diane duly triumphed, returning from a series of sobbing, chain-smoking family gatherings with photos of the two victims and a treasure chest of personal details. Everything her editor could have hoped for was there, from school nativity roles and sporting achievements to post-mortem results and funeral arrangements.

It was the story behind the story, the sort he himself had excelled at. His first staff appointment, the first female reporter in the *Bugle's* history, had been more than justified.

He pencilled it in as the front-page lead, relegating the official opening of the new road to a picture story: bad news sold newspapers.

Twenty-four hours to deadline and the front page was sewn up. That was how the editor liked it, just as Colin had, in the days when Simon the reporter longed for the week's best story to break just before deadline, so that it was piping-hot when the *Bugle* hit the streets. Back then, however, he wasn't the one with the printers and Walter Harding on his back, grumbling about late pages and overtime costs.

He went outside for a breath of fresh air and lit a Park Drive. His stomach growled in defiance of the ache in his jaw and he set off along High Street for Georgio's Café, the nearest eatery since Solly's Transport Café and Lodging House had been condemned by health inspectors.

The route took him past Beighton's newsagent's and the call from inside came like clockwork.

''Ere!'

Simon could never hear that voice without remembering Colin's description of its owner: 'tub-of-lard, chain-smoking mouth-almighty, breathless, red-faced, looks like he's been caught shagging the pet dog'.

'Heard about Mrs Jackson?' Eric barked.

'You've not been molesting old ladies again, have you, Eric?' Simon laughed.

'No, you prat, she's been burgled. So they tell me.'

Who 'they' were was anybody's guess: perhaps the beat bobbies who dropped in for their early morning cuppa as Eric sent his paper boys out on their rounds. 'They' were always telling Eric something in strictest confidence and he could not wait to tell someone else.

'Four thousand quid's worth of jewellery, they reckon,' he burbled. 'Ask the police, see if I'm right.'

Valerie Jackson was not only a magistrate but co-founder of the Neighbourhood Watch in her upmarket cul-de-sac, and Simon hurried back to the office with the story taking shape in his head: 'Crime-watch crusader Valerie Jackson was left wondering where all the nosey neighbours were this week when burglars stripped her home of valuables…'

He set his young protege on the story but Diane soon hit a brick wall. The usual police channels were saying nothing. Jackson raged about press intrusion and said she would be speaking to her lawyers if anything were published. Minutes later, her brother called from his furniture shop and threatened to withdraw his advertising.

In desperation, the editor called the nearest he had to a friend on the force, Detective Sergeant Kevin Feakes, whose mother's fruit scones had earned her honourable mentions in *Bugle* reports of village fetes. But even Feakes clammed up, refusing to confirm there had been a burglary in the (alleged) victim's street, much less say who the (alleged) victim was.

'Sorry, mate,' Feakes said, 'but there are times when victims insist on no publicity and we honour that, as a rule. Not,' he added with a chuckle, 'that I'm saying there was a victim here.'

Simon gave him a sulky lecture on the public's right to know how their money was being spent, adding that it was strange how only the rich or influential seemed to know about this right to anonymity.

It got him nowhere and he had to face facts: there were none. No story.

4

JIM Richardson had no doubt that the biggest single threat to society in the Britain of 1979 was illegal drugs.

The poison had seeped so deep that three out of every four house burglaries were committed in the name of drugs, the stolen goods being sold to handlers, who sold them on at car-boot sales to a public disinclined to question a bargain.

That the media was partly to blame, he also had no doubt. Serious TV programmes and full pages in national newspapers were devoted to the legalise-cannabis debate. Government ministers came out of smoke-filled closets to admit they had tried dope at college – but never inhaled, of course – in effect saying, 'It's all right, kids, I did it and look at me.'

Even among Richardson's police colleagues there was an element in favour of letting the druggies get on with it.

He had heard all the arguments for legalisation. There was no firm medical evidence against it, the supporters said. Decent people were being criminalised for a bit of harmless fun, they said. Marijuana led to hard drugs? Rubbish, they said. No more than a sip of beer led to a whisky-soaked alcoholic, they said.

Richardson thought they should try telling that to his brother's girl. Try telling Tanya it was harmless to be hit by two tons of steel at 60mph. Try telling her that never being able to walk again or be a ballet dancer or have children was fun. Try telling her that the driver who had been smoking heroin before he ploughed into her at a bus stop was a decent person really. Try telling her it was coincidence that his habit began with a spliff behind the school gym. Try telling her.

And where, he would ask with incredulity, did the legalise-it brigade think this 'harmless' herb came from? Some tax-paying member of the chamber of trade? Did they not realise that the men behind the men behind the street dealers were gangsters, the sort who specialised in concrete overcoats?

Back on his old patch, he was determined to make a difference. Getting up to speed on the players in the drug scene was a priority and, as he scanned the pages of the *Bugle* in search of familiar names, he noted that Simon Fox had gone up in the world.

'Mr Goody Two Shoes!' he muttered to himself.

The name had cropped up occasionally in address books seized in raids or in conversation with arrested druggies, who would try anything to get bail. Richardson would have given Fox a tug long ago but his superiors had held him back, fearing bad publicity if things went wrong.

He did not mention names when he set out his mission during a meeting with his new CID team. But he urged his detectives not to be fooled by outward appearances when investigating the drug scene.

'People in the media, local government, education,' he said, 'some of these are worse than the layabouts who shoot up in shop doorways. You know where you are with *them*. But intellectual types who like a few spliffs or a bit of powder at weekends are a more corrosive element: outwardly respectable but quietly subversive. They're the enemy within.'

*

HE had been back for just a week when he began to feel he had never left. Feakes was seated beside him in the interview room when Shane 'Flick' Beresford was brought in, looking more dishevelled than usual after a night in the cells.

'Well, what a surprise!' Richardson laughed. 'It's the proverbial bad penny.'

'Can't keep away, can yer?' Flick sneered. 'Thought I smelt summat.'

Richardson gave him a cold stare. 'Some things never change,' he said. 'Friday night comes round and some pissed-up little scrote who thinks he's hard goes sticking one on a kid about half his age.'

''Cept I ain't done nowt,' Flick snapped. 'It's a bloody fit-up, this.'

'Well then, Mr Beresford, would you like to give us your version of events, not that I'm expecting it to contain a grain of truth?'

'Come on now, Shane,' Feakes soothed. 'We can either play silly buggers and keep you banged up over the weekend, or you can cooperate and be out on bail this afternoon. Up to you. How's the injury, by the way?'

'How d'ya think?' Flick said, instinctively touching the badly scarred side of his face.

'Must be painful,' Feakes grimaced. 'Now, we know you were in the Unicorn at about 10pm last night and, according to several witnesses, you nutted a young bloke called Billy Jordan, causing a cut to his right eyebrow. Those same witnesses said it appeared to be a completely unprovoked and…'

'Unprovoked?' Flick cut in. 'The little twat were taking the piss. Anyroad, I didn't nut him.'

'So,' Richardson took over, 'are you denying that your forehead came into contact with his?'

'No but…'

'But what? A bit of magic at play, was it, Shane? Two foreheads collide, all of their own doing?'

Feakes chuckled. His boss was a smart-arse but an amusing one at times.

Flick smirked.

'Then tell us what happened. We're all ears.'

'Well, I'd been drinking wi' me mates…'

'That's a lie for a start,' Richardson laughed. 'You haven't got any mates!'

'Ha-fucking-ha. So, I'd been in there since about eight and there were no trouble at all. Then *Al Capone* comes on the jukebox and when it gets to "don't call me scarface" I hear laughing, like, and see this youth looking straight at me, so…'

'So,' said Richardson, 'you decide to teach him a lesson?'

'No! I goes over to him and says, calmly, like, "you got a problem, mate?" And next thing there's a push in mi back. Couple o' lairy lads behind me are dancing about a bit, and I gets sorta jerked forward and that's when I catch 'im wi' mi forehead. Simple as that. I never meant to nut him,' Flick grinned, 'otherwise he'd 'ave been out cold.'

'Ah, so it was an accident?' Richardson said wearily. 'Your forehead seems to have a knack of being involved in accidents, doesn't it? Like the time you nutted poor old Dr Chowdhury. OK. I've heard enough of this nonsense. Fetch me a charge sheet, Sergeant.'

'What?' Flick looked aghast. 'You gonna charge me? What wi?'

'Common assault, at least, possibly ABH. Either way, you're looking at two years, I reckon, what with the GBH on the doctor. Only did six months for that, didn't you? By my maths, you've still got 18 months suspended outstanding. So, add on six months for last night's little episode and...'

Flick sighed heavily but, as the door closed behind Feakes, Richardson leaned across and said softly, 'I might be able to make this go away, Shane.'

'Oh aye, and 'ow's that?'

'I might have one more little job for you.'

*

STONEWALLING the *Bugle* over that burglary had left Feakes uneasy. He prided himself on a good relationship with the local paper. Some of his colleagues would not give its young editor the time of day but Feakes had grown to trust him, enough to feed him information occasionally, even if only an off-the-record steer that might stop him making a fool of the paper and, more importantly, the police.

Besides, it paid to keep the press sweet. You never knew when you might need them.

The chance to make an offer of amends came sooner than he had expected. He phoned Simon's direct line.

'Sorry about that business the other day, mate.'

'Yeah, well that's life, Kev. Not the first time I've been shafted by the police and I don't suppose it'll be the last.'

'Don't be like that, you big girl,' the officer laughed. 'How'd you fancy coming on a job? I've got the OK to invite you along to see some real action, first-hand.'

'What sort of job?'

'Something to do with drugs. Cannabis, I think. But that's very hush-hush.'

Simon's stomach churned. What could he say? Thanks, but no thanks? I'm washing my hair that night? Or, I've got a Mothers' Union report to rewrite?

'Mmm, interesting,' he said. 'Locally, you mean?'

'Huh-huh. We're doing some raids on dealers and there's one coming up but no date yet. It'd probably be a case of giving you a bell just before we set off, then picking you up.'

'Sounds fun. Is this me personally, or just a reporter from the paper?'

'Up to you, mate. Send one of your minions if you like. That Diane seems a nice lass. I'd lend her my truncheon any time.'

'Give over, man! She's only 17.'

'Old enough to bleed, old enough to breed,' Feakes leered. 'Seriously, though, I thought you might fancy doing some real reporting again. That's if you're still up to it, after all the time you've spent hiding behind a desk. And my gaffer mentioned you. Always best to deal with someone you know, innit? Did you hear we've got a new DCI?'

'No, who's that?'

'Old mate of yours. Richo.'

*

TO their hard-working neighbours in Buttermere Drive, it was an outrage that benefit-scrounging Cyril Beresford enjoyed a luxury that some of them could not afford – a home telephone – let alone the freedom to lower the tone of the estate by keeping an old caravan in the back garden and fooling the council into believing it was merely for storage.

Its occupant was home on bail.

Friday night was family night, with bingo and chips, at the nearby community centre, and Flick waited for his parents and youngest sister to head out before letting himself into the house and making use of the phone. Better that than a trek up the street to a red box smelling of pee and littered with broken glass.

'Brexham CID,' Richardson answered.

'Listen,' said Flick, 'That guy I mentioned, he's in business.'

'You sure about that?' the inspector growled. 'You better not be pissing me about.'

'Please yersen,' said Flick. 'Couple o' mates was up there yesterday. Said he's got a big lump o' Moroccan. I asked one on 'em to tell him to save me some and…'

'And who might those mates be?'

'Fuck off! As if I'm gonna tell you that. Anyroad, I'm goin' round tomorrow, about 5ish. But if this goes tits-up, I tell yer I'll deny everything.'

'Don't worry, it won't. Just act naturally – and make sure you're clean when you go in. Right?'

'And the ABH? That'll go away.

'Trust me,' said Richardson.

5

WALTER Harding checked his whites for alien fluff and pulled the creases to attention.

He combed his rampant eyebrows and pipe smoker's moustache and patted the paunch that had turned him from all-round athlete to suet pudding before he had noticed, as if patting it might go away. It didn't, and he winced at precisely the moment he heard the clatter of ball on stumps once more on the field outside.

What shreds of fighting spirit and dreams of sporting glory lingered from his days as a useful all-rounder were funnelled into this match.

His Horizon paymasters had spotted the patently obvious: that there was little for him to do at the *Bugle* since the appointment of an advertising manager. When early retirement was offered, Walter accepted almost as swiftly as he turned down the offer of dinner at a posh hotel to mark his departure.

Instead, he suggested a farewell cricket match against a side captained by Harry Barkes, the boorish production director whose undisguised contempt for the *Bugle*'s old-fashioned ways, and Walter's cardigans, the MD had borne in angry silence since the day of the takeover.

Sensing the opportunity for some corporate bonding and a feature in the company magazine, Head Office agreed to pick up the bill and left Walter to make the arrangements.

It was years since Barkes had picked up a bat in anger but he was a company man through and through. He could hardly turn down the challenge.

Walter assembled a side from his friends among the town's shopkeepers and estate agents. He spent the moments before his call to the crease in the toilets of Brexham Town CC's cucumber sandwich and honeysuckle pavilion, steeling himself for what might be his final chance to star, while practising a nonchalant shrug of the shoulders that would say 'I did my best and it's only a game' if the unthinkable should happen.

Eighty-six for seven. Time for a captain's innings, he told the mirror, and marched out to the searing smile of a high sun and an outfield shimmering with several hues of green. Thunder flies mobbed him and a lark serenaded his arrival at the cracked, dusty square.

He might have hoped for a fairer game from Barkes but had not expected it. His enemy had bowled his best paceman without a break and an assortment of inswingers and vicious lifters had brought him 5-25, with Walter's ageing batsmen too busy protecting their bodies to worry about their wickets.

Walter tugged at the peak of his cap and looked around. It was an attacking field but it was there to be plundered. The prospect of fours over the fielders' heads to the short boundary was mouth-watering.

Head down. Bat tapping instep. Heart pounding.

The bowler arched in his delivery stride. Walter saw the ball pitch. He measured its pace. He followed its swing. He hooked towards mid-wicket... and heard the death rattle of his middle peg.

As he trudged back to the dressing room, a cry that sounded like 'banker' went up from his team-mates.

*

SIMON watched from the pavilion. Walter had tried talking him into playing and the prospect of turning his arm over for the first time since his school days as a demon bowler had been tempting but common sense had got the better of him and he had bowed to niggling back pain.

There was a phone call for him at the bar and he answered it half-expecting Diane Pickering to tell him there had been a fire or a murder. It was Kev Feakes.

'Simon! Couldn't get you at home, mate, so I tried your young lady reporter. She said you'd be there. Remember that job I was telling you about? Well, it's on this afternoon, mate. We'd have to pick you up about five?'

'What, on a Saturday?'

'The fight against crime waits for no man,' Feakes laughed.

'OK,' Simon said, unable to think of an excuse that seemed vaguely credible and suddenly seized by stomach ache.

By the time Feakes arrived, Barkes's team was heading for victory and Walter had dispatched himself to the farthest point from the bat, having seen his solitary over of leg spin bludgeoned for 18, including a huge six into the duck pond.

*

FEAKES was seated in the back of an unmarked Astra. Richardson was in the front, beside a driver introduced only as Minch, who appeared to have a large wooden pole between his legs.

Richardson greeted the editor like an old friend and promptly laid down the ground rules – Simon was to follow them in, take his pictures and say nothing – before talking about his strategy to combat the middle men, as he called them: regular dealers who handled pounds of cannabis, rather than ounces; quiet characters who stayed well away from the street scene.

'Take them out and you cut off the small fry, the scrotes who peddle two-quid deals to kids up town,' the chief inspector grinned as he turned to face Simon.

He had hoped for a trace of apprehension but found the editor busy checking the camera he had become adept at using, out of necessity since Horizon had made half of the group's photographers redundant.

Simon's outward calm disguised the maelstrom in his bowels. What if the target was someone he knew? He had visions of bursting in on someone he had smoked with, or even scored from. The poor sod might finger him there and then, and who could blame them? Soon, every copper in the county would know about the local newspaper editor's criminal connections, and his credibility would be lost.

*

WALTER'S cavalry arrived in the unlikely figure of Derek Potter, a beanpole of a furniture salesman with cold eyes.

Potter was no more than a useful medium-pacer but, dizzy on the blood of imminent victory, Barkes's men swung and swiped carelessly as Potter sent down a stream of good-length deliveries and engineered the sort of collapse that had become synonymous with English cricket.

The final over arrived with four runs needed and one wicket standing. Barkes was still in, and facing.

*

THE Astra entered a familiar estate of terrace houses. Simon's head was thumping. Please, he thought, don't let it be Stu.

It turned into Collingdale Street, home of his regular supplier.

'Oh shit!' he was thinking. 'Turn your brain on, Stu. I'm sending you a message. Get rid of it, quick!'

They stopped a few doors away. Stuart Miller's smart red BMW was parked down the street.

'A fucking 3 Series,' Minch muttered. 'I must be in the wrong job.'

'Now we wait,' Richardson said, his eyes fixed on Stu's front door. Feakes adjusted his tie. Minch gripped his sledgehammer.

A small, scrawny figure trailing a whippet on a length of rope ambled past in concertina jeans and Doc Martens.

'Here we go,' said Feakes.

The figure glanced furtively around and then vanished down the alley to Stu's back door. Even in the fading light, Simon recognised the barbecued features of Flick Beresford.

'Give him a few minutes,' Richardson said.

*

BARKES padded away the first ball of the final over, missed the second and strode down the wicket before the third left Potter's hand.

It was a head-back, eyes-closed, back-arched, sod-the-manual thrash of a shot. The ball soared high towards long-on, where Walter waited on tiptoes, hands cupped. This was it, the moment of salvation. Please, God, he thought, don't let me drop it. Don't let me look a prat again.

Bollocks! Where's it gone?

He squinted at the sun for what seemed like minutes, waiting for the tiny dot to be spat back out. When next he saw it, it was several feet to his right, just above shoulder height and hurtling towards the boundary rope.

Walter would never tire of recounting what happened next: how he spun on arthritic knees, how he launched into a goalkeeper's dive, how the ball bounced with a sickening crack off his thumb but how he grasped it safely at the second attempt, barely a foot off the ground, and how his fall to earth winded him so severely that his ecstatic team-mates had to carry him off.

*

FLICK paused inside the alleyway. Go inside, buy the gear and stay there as long as you can. That was the deal.

Fuck that, he thought.

'Shush, boy,' he whispered as he picked up Monty and padded silently across Stuart Miller's back garden. They were over the small fence and away before the officers reached the house.

The raiding party arrived at the front door. Richardson could see the flicker of a television behind closed curtains. He knocked twice, shouting, 'This is the police, Mr Miller. Open the door!'

Simon stood out of sight, hands shaking as he aimed the camera. Richardson counted slowly to five, then nodded to Minch. Two hammer blows crashed the door open and they were in, trampling through Stu's front room, yanking open the dividing door, storming into the very lounge where Simon had sat and smoked and done business with his old friend.

And then came a sound he had never heard from a hippy with a beard. It was the scream of an old lady.

The camera flashed at the white-haired figure of Olive Miller, clinging to the corner of a table, her free hand waving a walking stick in a feeble gesture of defiance, watery eyes set to pop, mouth open in a desperate attempt to draw breath. Then it flashed again at the stunned face of Jim Richardson.

*

UNTIL the moment he had stepped into the alley, Flick had been in two minds. Then, suddenly, he knew what to do.

'One more little job then I'll be off your back,' Richo had said, 'and the assault charge will go away.'

Yeah, like he could trust a copper.

No one could imagine the pain he was in. He had been scarred for life by the barbecue incident. Not that Richo gave a damn. Hadn't gone out to see how he was. None of them had. Flick had been left to call his own ambulance. The police had not even taken a statement from Wagga.

There was only one thing for it.

'We're outta this place, old friend,' he said, filling a bowl of water for his breathless pet as they reached their caravan home.

Inside, he found his rucksack with its sewn-on Rolling Stones tongue logo and crammed it full of what clean clothes he could find, along with two cans of Skol lager, a portable cassette player, a small lump of hashish wrapped in tinfoil, and a tape of the Sex Pistols' *Never Mind the Bollocks*.

With almost all his worldly goods slung over his shoulder, he strode out for the nearest bus stop with Monty in tow. He thought he might ring his folks later; he might not.

Of one thing he was sure: he'd had it with Brexham. He had no real friends left, no chance of building a relationship with Lucy now that her mum had moved to Skegness, no chance of picking up decent birds, not with a face like something from a horror movie.

And always in the background, like Old Nick on his shoulders, was Richo, the one man who knew his big secret and who would now be out to lock him up.

Then there was Stu. Richo might tell him who'd set him up, then the mad Scotsman would be after him for being a grass.

He'd make a fresh start, that's what he'd do. Or at least have a change of scenery. His old mucker Colley was living on a narrowboat down Coventry way. They hadn't met up for ages but Colley had told him to drop by any time.

A good lad, was Colley. They'd had some wild times together. Flick chuckled at the memory of the night they went into a chippie and Colley asked the young assistant if they battered sausages and when she said 'yes', he flobbed his dick on the counter and said 'well, batter this!'

Colley had never worked, as far as Flick was aware, but he always managed to get by. Loved his foraging. Amazing what he could cook up with stuff out of hedgerows. And always managed to pick up some fine blow on his travels.

The bus stopped on the outskirts of town and dog and master jumped off. A half-mile walk took them to the M1 junction, where Flick held Monty in his arms and struck up his best hitchhiker pose. They had not waited long when an Eddie Stobart wagon pulled up.

Flick kissed his pet on the lips and scampered towards the open door. Climbing aboard, he turned to face the town of his birth and yelled, 'Ta-rar, shithole!'

*

THE summons to Force Headquarters for a meeting with Assistant Chief Constable Bernie Wormald was inevitable. Mrs Miller had instructed solicitors.

Kev Feakes had done his best to dissuade his editor friend but the story had made the *Bugle*'s front page, with the old lady's furious comments alongside a picture of DCI Richardson and the headline 'DRUGS RAID BUNGLE'.

Wormald had the paper in front of him.

'We'll make it go away but it'll cost us,' he scowled.

Richardson sighed, head bowed

'I presume you got their door fixed, Jim.'

'First thing next morning, sir.'

'And nothing in the house to incriminate this man of yours?'

'Not a speck. He'd been careful.'

'Shame. But it is what it is.'

'I can only apologise, sir. Thought my intel was cast-iron.'

'Huh! No such thing, Jim. But you're not the first copper to be caught out that way and you won't be the last. I don't want it to put you off your mission – I know how important this is to you – but we can't afford another cock-up like this.'

'No, sir. I've learned a painful lesson, believe me.'

'I do, Jim, which is why I'm marking this down as "advice given" on your file.'

Richardson smiled nervously. 'I'm grateful, sir. I won't let you down.'

'Good, good. But erm…'

'Sir?'

'Put the raids on hold, OK? I want no more for a couple of months. Keep gathering your intel but consult me before you go breaking any more doors down.'

Richardson gave his word and left, silently vowing retribution on Flick Beresford, wherever he might be.

He would never know that his 'cast-iron' intelligence had been undone by a chance phone call on the day before the raid.

Stuart Miller's cousin Liam, not long out of jail for dealing and looking to resume his career, had phoned from Glasgow.

In his excitement, Stu forgot all about Flick's visit as he buried an old biscuit tin containing his dealer kit on his allotment and drove to Scotland with a lump of sandy-coloured hash the size of a paperback novel in the glove compartment, terrified at the prospect of being stopped by the police but gleeful at the thought of offloading all that gear in one go.

He arranged for his mother to look after the cats while he was gone and borrowed his father's brown Volvo. Much less conspicuous than the Beamer.

He planned to stay for just the night but found himself being dragged along next day to Liam's mate's wedding reception, where Liam spent the evening having the mickey taken out of his second-hand suit, his hair and his earrings by the groom's grandfather.

Liam exacted revenge with a hefty pinch of hash in the old man's pipe while he was at the bar.

They hung around long enough to watch grandad being helped to a taxi, racked by spasms of bronchial laughter, and returned to Liam's house to find a hysterical message from Stu's mum on the answerphone.

6

THE uneasy peace between editor and production director ended on the day Simon discovered, two hours before the paper was due on the press, that he had an extra page to fill. An advertiser had dropped out and no one had bothered to tell the editor.

'How am I supposed to plan when there's no communication?' he stormed at Harry Barkes. 'If you want me to keep producing a decent paper, I need more staff.'

'Try making the pictures and headlines bigger,' Barkes sneered. 'And stop trying to squeeze in every farting little bit of news.'

'What he's saying, in effect,' Simon told Lynne later, 'is, "You're a fool for doing what you've been doing for so long, pack it in."'

'Well then,' she said, 'perhaps you should.'

He had huffed and puffed about leaving many times before. But this was different. Something stirred deep inside, so deep that it could not be ignored, like the knowledge that one more beer would have him honking into the toilet bowl, though that rarely stopped him. It was that deep-down knowledge of oneself that might defy everyone else's logic and even one's own in the cold light of day, but which raged in the hot sweat of sleepless nights, screaming to be heard.

That evening, he called Gary Bostock at the *Evening Gazette*. 'They're always after subeditors,' said his former colleague. 'It might suit you, taking your foot off the gas for a while.'

Four days later, he was driving back from a job interview.

He turned the Stranglers up loud on the car radio and lost himself in images of life flashing by on inter-city streets: pigeons fighting over scraps outside a chip shop; babies in pushchairs gurning at each other as their mothers smoked and gossiped; a young black girl skipping in and out of a length of elastic stretched between the legs of two white friends.But there was no hushing the hurricane inside. He had a decision to make and all he wanted to do was hide from it.

They WANTED him. THEY wanted him. They wanted HIM.

Walking through the *Gazette's* open-plan newsroom, full of serious faces staring at computer screens, he had felt like a schoolboy summoned to see the headmaster.

Editor Phil Smythe, a stocky, shaven-headed man, was renowned for his explosive temper and his penchant for hiring journalists based on their breast size or a willingness to play for the paper's five-a-side football team.

According to Gary, the morning editorial conferences, where senior staff reviewed the latest edition and put forward ideas for the next, were known as 'The Crucifixion', and Smythe had once got so furious with a mild-mannered writer that he had bounced himself off his office walls while shouting 'fuck, fuck, fuck!'

Simon found him charm personified.

Smythe seemed more concerned with what they could offer him than what he could do for them.

Could he take orders, the editor wondered. After all, he was used to being his own boss. Wouldn't he be frustrated as an untitled 'sub', editing stories and making headlines fit someone else's page plans? Wouldn't he miss the freedom to do and write more or less what he pleased?

It would be difficult, Simon acknowledged, but he was sure he could adapt.

Besides, the idea of being master of one trade, instead of pulling himself in all directions as a small-town jack of all, had a certain appeal.

He knew that if he stayed much longer at the *Bugle*, he might be seen as being too stuck in his ways to ever make the move to a bigger paper.

He could start his new role whenever he wished, the editor had said. The pay would just about cover the loss of his company car but the hours were shorter – and regular – and the holidays longer, and he would have to take them: none of the *Bugle's* odd-days-off-in-lieu nonsense.

Simon promised to let him know within the week.

As he neared the comfort blanket of his little hometown with its little newspaper, he wondered if he was crazy to even consider the offer; to give up the status of editor, of big fish in small pond – local celebrity, boss of his own domain.

Perhaps.

But so much fun had gone out of the job and he could see himself a few years down the line: a grumpy, twisted, middle-aged hack, unhappy in his work but for ever striving to maintain unrealistic standards that might one day send a searing pain through his chest and lay him out across his desk.

Some might say he should stay and fight, that to leave now would show he couldn't hack it in the modern era. But he could look them in the eye and say he had given it his best shot, and at least he would be going at the top, when people would ask 'why?' rather than waiting for them to say, 'Isn't it time you left?'

What began as a job had become a drug. There would be withdrawal symptoms, for sure. He wondered how he would cope with driving past the office at weekends without popping in to open the mail.

What would become of his evenings, with no stories to take home to edit?

How would he dodge the decorating, the gardening and all those other jobs Lynne had let him put off because he was too busy with his work?

How would he survive in public settings without his Bugle Man cape to pull on and make himself important?

*

IGNORING the taunts of passing schoolboys, Eddie Thacker checked his makeup in a shop window and strode confidently down High Street.

The backlash from the trial had been awful. He was innocent, and wounded, disabled, in fact, for the injury caused occasional spasms in his right arm, yet people had sneered at him in the streets as if he'd actually killed Tommy Jepson.

True, the old man might not have died without all the aggravation, but that was hardly Eddie's fault. He had just been taking a leak when a sword was stuck in his arm. But the abuse had got even worse when it emerged that he had been paid £1,000 by the Criminal Injuries Board

In some ways, though, the aftermath had been the jolt he needed. He had enrolled at night school and spent his spare time studying instead of boozing.

Four O-levels led to a job on the check-in desk at the region's airport, and there he made friends with young people far removed from the roughhouse, macho culture of his old crowd.

In that more liberal environment, Eddie gradually came to terms with feelings which, he finally understood, had been hidden in shame since he was a child and submerged in drink, drugs and bravado in adulthood.

Months of agonising, of looking at length in a mirror and asking himself what he wanted to be, how he wanted to live, eventually brought clarity. A momentous change was required, one from which he could never draw back.

But now, as he reached his destination, he hesitated and lit a cigarette. Knowing what he wanted to do was one thing. Telling the world about it was a prospect that made his stomach churn.

*

THE faces of two-bit villains flashed through Simon's head as he drove past the town's courthouse. He remembered how Colin had laughed when Simon had told him their names, for the editor had covered their fathers' petty crimes when they were young and were represented by lawyers whose sons went on to plead for the next generation of law-breakers.

So many memories. The court usher's father was a former mayor. Her son sent cricket reports to the *Bugle*. His neighbour was a dustman who claimed to have discovered the secret of perpetual motion in his garage. Nearby lived an amateur footballer who was playing in a match when police marched him off the field for murdering his mother. Around the corner lived a postman and his alcoholic wife. Having accidentally burnt their house down one Christmas Eve, she had confessed all to the kindly reporter, grateful for his help in getting her senile father into a nursing home after his dementia had led to him defecating in the kitchen sink, causing nasty stains in the flat below. Just a few of the raw, joyous, tragic, caring, brutal, vibrant lot that made up *Bugle* readers.

And he might soon be leaving them.

How would he cope with being a nobody? No more suffering every Tom, Dick and Harry every time he went out for a pint, just in case they came in useful one day? No more 'could you get a photographer to our coffee morning?'; 'would you mind taking an advert into the office?'; or the ubiquitous 'I could tell you a story but you wouldn't dare print it!'

185

If all the threads that bound him to that role were snapped, would he fall apart? Without the connections that made him more than a face in the crowd, would he join the undead, floating miserably around the honeypot of local life, running cold fingers down familiar faces but never being seen?

For now, though, such weighty considerations had to be put on hold. He had a newspaper to get out and was comforted by the knowledge that a front-page lead was in the bag: an update on the life of little Daniella Wojcik, though not so little now, as the latest photograph from her proud grandmother showed.

Krystyna's own transformation had been extraordinary. She now worked on the tills at Fine Fare, had become an enthusiastic churchgoer and was, she vowed, off the booze for good.

The change in Daniella was even more remarkable. Just two years after her operation, the tall, healthy-looking girl at her school sports day looked nothing like the sickly child whose picture had inspired *Bugle* readers to give her a new life.

Yes, Simon thought: a good-news front page would make a refreshing change.

He was no sooner through the office door than Celia Staunton was at his side, twittering breathlessly. The veteran receptionist's noddy-dog head shook slightly more to the left than right, indicating a solitary figure at the desk where customers sat to write out their Classified ads.

'That, erm,' Celia whispered, 'that gentleman has been waiting for an hour. He used to be a teddy boy but he says he wants to…'

'What's up, Celia?'

Her cheeks were crimson. Every decent bone in her body defied her to continue. 'He's wearing lipstick and eye shadow and… erm, he says he's going to have a sex-change operation. He wants to know if you'd like to print a story. I told him I didn't think you'd be interested but…'

Simon's stomach churned with excitement. This was *News of the World* stuff.

'Send him through!' he beamed. 'I'll see him myself.'

As his visitor was shown in and took a seat, the editor thought the face looked vaguely familiar.

'So,' he said gently as he reached for a notepad, 'I gather you have an interesting story to tell me. Can I get some basic details first?'

'Yeah, sure.'

'Good. Let's start with your name?'

'Edwina.'

Simon's eyebrows rose.

'Well, that's what I prefer to be called and I'm going to change my name by deed poll eventually…'

'OK,' Simon cut in, 'so I'll call you Edwina while we're chatting but I need to know your proper name as well.'

'It's Eddie, well, Edward really. Edward Thacker.'

The penny dropped with a clang and, in a flash, young Daniella's progress was demoted to an inside page as a headline formed in the editor's mind: 'SWORD HORROR VICTIM'S SEX-CHANGE DREAM'.

Yet another *Bugle* exclusive was on the way.

He was thinking he might stay after all.

CHAPTER FIVE

SIMON Fox had been in his new job for almost a year when he discovered the eighth wonder of the world. His son was born.

It had not been planned. Momentous changes in his life rarely were, and having someone else's teenaged children to look after from day one of their marriage had left him and Lynne with no appetite to follow their friends and get the baby bit out of the way so that they could enjoy life later.

Later was for other people. Once Dawn and Paul were off their hands, they relished being carefree.

Yet there was an inevitability about it. Lynne had always been so natural and at ease with children, always cradling babies at christenings and whooping around with nieces and nephews at family gatherings, while Simon shrank into the safety of adult conversation, fearful of being handed something that was sure to tense from head to toe and bawl for relaxed arms as he tried, with growing embarrassment, to pull funny faces and talk Baby.

The new era had its dawn in ten minutes of passion, unbridled – on the one and only occasion during Lynne's three-month health break from the Pill – by a condom, the sexual equivalent, as he put it, of wellington boots on a sun-baked beach.

A miscarriage at ten weeks thrust them into the greatest non-Masonic lodge of all, a world of aunts and cousins and women in corner shops who couldn't wait to open their closets and tell how they had endured the same ordeal and come through it.

Having begun the process of readjustment in their minds, with no real concept of the awesome task ahead, they decided to try again.

For 36 weeks, Lynne ballooned in size and blossomed in character. It was the laughter that did her in the end. Convulsed with giggles as Simon sang 'whale meet again' and rested his head on the lump that had taken to carrying her around on its back, she wet the bed, realised what it meant and dashed for the suitcase that stood, packed, at the foot of the stairs.

Six hours later, on the longest night of their lives, she was wheeled from an operating theatre, flat out on a trolley, her nightie soaked with perspiration and stained with blood around the stitches where they had carved her open, hugging the pink, hairy creature who had just ended one incredible journey and was about to begin another.

Simon stroked her hair and choked 'I love you', tears streaming down his face as he stood, childlike, in a sea of white coats and stethoscopes, all inhibitions washed away in a salty stream let loose more by relief that his soulmate had survived than by joy at the wonder of creation.

Time was tipped on its head. It could have been seconds or hours later that a nurse entered the waiting room, smiling, a baby in her arms, and he wondered: what now? This was all new. He supposed he should reach out but hesitated. Was it his? Or was she just passing through with someone else's baby in her pocket?

She handed it to him and he was gripped by fear, wondering if he would pass the first test, afraid that he might freak out and drop it.

Beneath his rational, caring facade, was there a beast waiting for its moment to strike? A vision of him tossing the baby out of the window there and then flashed through his mind.

'Here you are, dad,' the nurse beamed.

He took it in his arms so gingerly he could have mixed it with whisky, and pulled its screwed-up face to his chest. It was truly wonderful. But was it all there? What if it was deformed? He had not dared to think of that. He looked at where the hands should be and saw two tiny fans of wax tapers that looked almost transparent and felt like nothing on earth.

The nurse read his thoughts. 'He's got all his fingers and toes and everything's all right,' she said, and at that moment he would have voted for any politician who promised nurses whatever they asked for.

He was thinking, 'Forgive me, baby, for being so sweaty. My arms aren't usually this stiff, you'll see. It's just that I'm petrified.'

He bent to plant a kiss on its pink forehead and whispered, 'Hello, little man. Aren't you just gorgeous?'

He talked to himself all the way home. All tests paled beside this one. He had wasted so many things – money, belongings, friends, opportunities – but this was a one-off. There were no second sittings at the Examination of Parenthood. Screw this up and he'd have a juvenile delinquent on his hands.

He was in at the start, on virgin territory. And had he not always said that people were what they were made, not born with? There could be no one else to blame if he queered this pitch.

Somewhere in the roar of confusion there was another, quieter voice. It was telling him not to panic. Being a dad, it was saying, was the most natural thing in the world. He'd be fine. Look at what he'd survived in the past! If any poor, ignorant peasant in the jungle could do it, if some battered and abused lad on a council estate with none of his wealth and clever ideas could cope, surely he could, too?

But he was not convinced.

*

SO began the greatest adventure of his life.

In the months and years ahead, little Tom Fox swept his parents on a voyage for which they had been woefully ill-prepared. Someone should write the definitive book about it, Simon would say, because no one told you what it was *really* like. He might have done it himself but was too busy living the story; too busy coochy-cooing and giggling and snuggling up to his perfect toy.

'What's it like to be a dad?' people asked, and he wanted to say: what's it like to be alive? It was the bee's knees, brilliant to the power of a million, the jewel in every crown, the thing that came before sliced bread.

'Lovely,' he'd say, chuckling and gooey-eyed. And when his friends in the pub were discussing football or TV or lusting over some young woman across the room, all he wanted to talk about was Tom.

Look at the state of you, said the devil inside. Is this what you've been reduced to? There was a brain in your head once upon a time. It grappled with great issues. It moralised and theorised. It spawned sparkling conversation and wicked wit. Now look at you! Is this the height of your ambition?

And it was.

He remembered how he would cringe when old ladies at bus stops peered into prams and pulled gummy smiles while they tickled a baby's ribs and trilled that he looked like his dad but he'd got his mum's nose and did he sleep all right, and wait until he got older and then the trouble would start.

Now, they were doing it to his baby and all he could do was stand there with a big grin, basking in the glory, a star in a great show.

Tom's arrival had burst a dam that had held back his emotions since the day his mother died. So all-consuming had been the task of survival that he had cloaked himself in an armour of responsibility from which he only rarely, and secretly, escaped.

He had immersed himself in work to the point where he needed chemical stimulation to ease the pressure – and then had to work like fury the next day to get the fog out of his head, and so on. Fearful of getting hurt, he had kept all but a tight group of his most trusted friends at arm's length.

Now, he gorged himself on tactile pleasures. Life as a subeditor on the *Evening Gazette* had brought long, lazy evenings back into his life, and he spent them smelling Tom's scalp, kissing the back of his neck, nibbling his toes, burying a stubbly chin in his belly, making him kick and chuckle, and looking into those cavernous, brown, wonder-filled eyes as he held him above his head and caught a snake of milky saliva on his lips.

He found himself laughing as he had not laughed for years, as pureed vegetables were scooped out by little fingers that flicked and flailed and rubbed themselves in hair and on furniture, and a voice that once could only scream in desperate hunger now sought to make sense of life's mysteries with questions like 'lar lar bob?'

He cried a lot, too; not when writing about real people being maimed on the roads or in pub brawls, but at soppy films and TV programmes. When Tom was old enough for his first visit to the cinema, it was Simon who emerged tearful from *Bambi*.

It was as if, like his son, he was being exposed to emotions for the first time.

Life had a purpose once more and the idea that he might die at 40 was just one of those ridiculous things he wished he had never thought, in case the thought made it happen.

Challenge reared up at him around every corner, forcing him on to his mettle, demanding the best, just as it had in the grief-ridden days after his parents died; just as it did ten minutes from deadline with 300 words to write.

Victories came in torrents: against the evil backache of winding Tom after his 3am feed, or shopping with him in one arm and two carrier bags on the other; against the dread of embarrassment at playgroup parties and school concerts; against bilious battles with nappy-splats, beds full of hot sick and the first grazed knees and torn fingers of his daring little adventurer, who had everywhere to run and climb and not a warning light in sight.

But between the chores and horrors there were sights and sounds to savour, from Tom's first encounter with the seaside, where rushing waves and vanishing sand below his feet made him so dizzy that he fell, chubby chops down, into the mush; to squeals of joy on helter-skelter rides, to mud-and-worm pies on paddling pool summer days, to first knock-kneed steps, to tree climbing, to Santa Claus and the Tooth Fairy.

When the best thing Simon had ever read came on a birthday card addressed to 'My Daddy' in Tom's own writing, he knew he was a fully fledged member of Big Softies Incorporated.

And he wouldn't have it any other way.